Copyright Info For Scars, Sins & Secrets by Lisa Gaiter

Created by Coach Tia Monique & Let It Out Academy©
Linktr.ee/Coachtiamonique

ABOUT THE AUTHOR:

Lisa Gaiter balances life in many roles as a dedicated mother, wife, leader, career professional and an entrepreneur. She is an avid reader who has taken interest in all phases of writing.

From storytelling, to writing a business plan or a proposal, you name it. Her passion is sharing stories in hopes that it will help someone who has the same or similar experiences.

DEDICATION

I dedicate this book to God,
My Grandmother who raised me to be the woman
I am today, my loving children, family and
real friends who keep me encouraged always!

table of contents

CHAPTER ONE

SCARS OF CHILDHOOD

It takes more than a wish to have a perfect life, to have a family that cares, and parents who courageously pull through to provide their children with the basic needs of life. Unfortunately, my lot in life was far from easy. My scars are the embodiment of years of struggle and excruciating pain, testaments to the battles I fought and won.

My name is Jade Allyson, and I was born and bred on the East Side of Detroit, Michigan. Growing up, my community was notorious for crimes and vices, and my small family of five, including my parents and two younger siblings, Jeffrey and Julian had to navigate the chaos every day.

Even amidst the turmoil, my family was my rock, my haven in hell. While the streets were crowded with hoodlums and each dawn brought new misfortunes, we had each other to hold onto.

Sometimes, I find myself reminiscing about my childhood, envying the days when I could watch the sunset on the horizon without a tinge of guilt or regret. I miss the dawns when I used to listen to the sweet songs of chirping birds and the distant sounds of cockerels announcing the arrival of a new day. As a child, I loved watching birds fly out of their nests and found a strange harmony in the bustling sounds of a busy street mixed with the sounds of nature.

Being just a kid, it was easy to lose one's way in the labyrinths of the Detroit slums. I was innocent and naive, having seen so little of the vast world, and the harsh realities of life in the ghetto bred mediocrity. How could it be any different in a place so littered with cartels, gangsters, prostitutes, and destitute people who had taken to the streets for rescue and survival?

Many young boys my age had already been initiated into dangerous criminal groups, running smart errands for

while young girls were indoctrinated into the long-standing tradition of prostitution. The overwhelming avalanche of corruption around me threatened to crush my fragile wall of defense, and when life took a turn for the worse, I found myself struggling to cope.

My dad, however, was a steadfast anchor in the midst of the stormy sea that was our neighborhood. His unwavering dedication to providing for our family was palpable in every fiber of his being. I remember how his calloused hands would still manage to gently lift me up, as if I weighed nothing at all. He was my protector, my hero.

No matter how exhausted he was from his long hours at the auto factory, he always managed to make time for us. I could hear the weariness in his voice, but it was always laced with love and tenderness. His presence brought a sense of calm to our cramped apartment, as if everything was going to be alright as long as he was there.

The crack of dawn was never an obstacle for my dad. He was always up before the sun, ready to face the challenges that awaited him at work. Sometimes, I would stir in my sleep and catch a glimpse of him getting ready in the dim light. His face was already lined with fatigue. He never complained, never once hinted at the weight of his responsibilities.

Sundays were the only days he could afford to rest. He would make the most of them, soaking up the precious moments of peace with his family. We would lounge around the living room, basking in the glow of our little television set, or venture outside to feel the warmth of the sun on our skin. And through it all, my dad was there. His presence was a constant reminder of the love that bound us together.

My mother's beauty was beyond skin deep. It was the inner strength that shone through her eyes, the resilience in her spirit, and the unwavering hope in her heart. Despite the

Our small apartment was a sanctuary amidst the chaos of the city. My father's long hours at the auto factory were a testament to his unwavering dedication to providing for our family. His broad shoulders and deep, reassuring voice gave us a sense of safety and security, even in the toughest of times.

My mother's optimism was contagious too. We all eagerly awaited the day when she would finally graduate from nursing school and start practicing. We hoped that her determination and hard work would lead to a brighter future for all of us.

Living in a two-bedroom apartment meant that we had to learn how to live in close quarters. My siblings, Jeffrey and Julian, were the noisiest, but also the most loving. Despite their constant bickering, they were each other's closest allies. Watching them play together filled our little home with joy and laughter.

My mother's cooking was always a highlight, and we would savor every bite. Afterwards, we would settle down in the living room to watch a movie or our favorite TV show.

As the sun began to set, we would often venture outside to take in the fresh air. Jeffrey and Julian, would run around in the open pavement, chasing each other and giggling uncontrollably. These were the moments that made our family bond stronger, and helped us forget, even if just for a moment, the struggles of living in the slums.

The day when everything changed, the air was thick with tension as my father arrived home on a Wednesday afternoon - an unusual occurrence. I stood frozen in the doorway, my body rigid with shock as I watched him slowly make his way into the house. His face was etched with pain, his eyes bloodshot and filled with a sadness that seemed to engulf him.

"Welcome Dad," I said with my voice shaky as I tried to mask my confusion.He barely acknowledged my greeting and his defeated tone cut through the silence. *"Where is your mom?"* he asked with his eyes scanning the room.

I told him she had just returned and was in the kitchen. He dropped his bag on the chair and walked straight to join her, leaving a trail of sadness and despair behind him. The once vibrant atmosphere quickly turned to one of dejection, leaving my brothers to pick up on the gravity of the situation as they retreated early to bed that night.

As the days passed, it became evident that something was terribly wrong. My father's absence from work was the least of our worries. The sadness that had enveloped him seemed to be taking over our entire household, casting a pall over everything we did. Even the air felt heavy, as though it was carrying a burden that we couldn't quite understand.

For days, my father was a shadow of his former self. He would sit on the old armchair, his gaze fixed on the peeling paint on the walls, lost in thought. His broad shoulders were slumped and his eyes were puffy and red from sleepless nights. I could tell that he was going through a tough time, and it broke my heart to see him in such a state.

I later learned that he was fired from his job without any warning or explanation. It was a cruel blow, especially for someone as dedicated and hardworking as my dad. He had given his all to the auto factory, working six days a week, and sacrificing time with his family to ensure that we had food on the table and a roof over our heads.

Life has a way of throwing curveballs when we least expect it. Our family was already in a precarious financial situation, and my father's sudden job loss only made things worse. My mom, being a nursing student at the time, was already struggling to pay for her school fees.

As if that wasn't enough, our landlord was constantly breathing down our necks, threatening to evict us if we didn't pay our rent. The pressure was intense, and it weighed heavily on my father's shoulders. Despite his efforts, things were spiraling out of control, and it seemed like there was no end in sight.

Something was really wrong and dad's behavior became more erratic. He would come home late at night, smelling of alcohol and cigarette smoke, and would disappear for days on end without telling us where he was going or when he would be back. Strange visitors kept coming, more and more frequently, and their appearance became more menacing with each passing day.

Men with hardened expressions and ominous auras would come knocking at our door at all times during the day. Their visits were growing more frequent everyday. One evening, as I sat in the living room, the doorbell rang. I glanced at my mother, who wore a troubled expression with lines of worry all over her face. My father, oblivious to the mounting tension, casually got up to answer the door.

As he swung the door open, I caught a glimpse of the man standing outside. He was tall, with a fearsome aura. I strained to hear their conversation because I knew something was wrong. I had to find out for myself what it was since my parents tried very hard to keep things from us.

"*Boss is losin' his mind, man. He ordered me to come get his cash from your last consignment.*" the man said. His voice was low and sounded very dangerous.

"*Yo, fam, I got you. I'll get the money for the boss real soon. I had to handle some urgent family business, you feel me? Just give me a lil' more time, aight?.*" The man's eyes narrowed cause his patience was wearing thin.

"*Bruh, you been talkin' that same crap for weeks now. Boss been showin' you mad patience, my nigga. You really don't wanna be the one makin' him lose that patience, ya feel me?*

Remember what happened to TJ and Izzy when they was rollin' with them niggas? You don't wanna end up in that same spot, man."

"I hear you, man. I'm puttin' in all my effort, I swear. I'll make sure that cash gets to the boss ASAP. Just give me a little more time, fam," dad said in pleading whispers.

"Your best ain't cuttin' it no more. Boss needs that money by the end of the week, or stuff is gonna hit the fan, straight up. Consequences gonna come knockin' if you don't step it up."

Fear gripped my heart as I heard my dad yell out, "Ouch!" The man had hit him in the head with something. I'm thinking that it was a gun because I rushed to help my mom help him up and there was blood dripping from the top of his hairline, down the side of his face. The guy vanishes into the distance, swallowed by the gloom of descending twilight.

My mom screams out, "Honey, are you okay? What is really going on? Should I call the police?"

"No! You can't call the police, and you know that."
However, the fear was evident in my mother's eyes. She had
overheard the conversation with the stranger. It was
impossible to ignore. She tightly clasped her hands together
with her anxiety visible. She was fully aware of the threat
the stranger had posed to my father.

"So now what are we gonna do?" She asked. My father
brushed aside her concerns. *"I'll figure something out. I
always do. Can you fix my head? Put some of your training
to work."* He tried to chuckle but my mother's lips never
cracked a smile.

The tension between my parents weighed heavily on my
little heart as I imagined the consequences of his
entanglement with the strange man. Their once
unbreakable bond was now strained. There was a delicate
thread threatening to snap under the weight of secrets.
Each day brought forth a new wave of arguments and
painful confrontations.

One night, I watched my mother sink into the worn-out couch with her eyes a reflection of worry and disappointment. She was sitting and rocking as my father paced around with his face wrinkled with the burden of his bad dealings.

"Please, you have to put an end to this," my mother pleaded with her voice quivering with sadness. *"I'm doing what needs to be done,"* he replied, *"Our family needs the money. I'm trying to provide for us."*

"But at what cost? Look at what it's doing to us! Look at what it's doing to you!"

Her gaze shifted towards the cluttered coffee table that was now loaded with bags of drugs and stacks of cash. *"I am so scared right now babe."* My mother walked up to him and put her arms around his waist like they used to do while playing around or dancing. This time it didn't make me smile. Tears began rolling down my face.
I ran to my bedroom and closed the door.

Their voices escalated, the echoes of their heated disagreement reverberating within the walls. My mother sounded angry at first and then she started whining, begging and pleading. However, Dad remained consumed by his own fears. He must've tried to walk away because his voice sounded farther away from mom.

"I'm doing this for us," he whispered, barely audible. "One day, we will have everything we have ever dreamed of."

With those words hanging in the air, I could sense that these recurrent disputes had struck at the very core of their love, leaving a fracture that would require more than mere words to mend.

Day after day, I could see the cracks forming in my father's facade. The strain of our precarious situation was wearing him down, even if he refused to admit it. The strange visitors, their horrific demands, and my mother's growing worry were fearful signs. The strange visits from the intimidating men continued.

Their demands grew more insistent, their threats more explicit. My father would disappear for hours, sometimes days, leaving our family in a state of constant anxiety.

He came back home one evening and he looked exhausted. His demeanor was filled with an unspoken unease. *"Dad, what's going on? Who are these men? Why do they keep coming?"* I had worried so long in silence and was longing for answers, I decided to speak up even if my voice was filled with concern.

My father's eyes met mine, I could tell he was shocked by my questions. He whispered, *"I got involved with the wrong people, Jade. I made some bad decisions to try and provide for our family. I thought I could handle it, but it's spiraling out of control."*

My heart sank at my father's confession. I could tell he needed someone to talk to but he was alone and felt helpless in the maze in which he had lost his way. I could see the weight of guilt and regret weighing heavily on him.

I reached out and took his hand so that my touch could be a silent reassurance that I was there for him.

"I'm so sorry, Jade."

"Dad, I'm sure that you will figure it out. You always do." I knew that I couldn't actually help but what I could do was let him know that I was confident in him no matter what.

Everything seemed to be going on fine for a while. Mom was finally able to continue her studies, but the road to recovery was not easy, especially for my father.

It wasn't until that fateful evening when everything changed permanently. We were all gathered in the living room when the phone rang. My heart sank as my mother answered, and I could tell by the look on her face that something was terribly wrong.

"Is this Mrs. Allyson?" the voice on the other end asked.

My mother confirmed her identity, and then the words that followed shattered our world.

"I'm sorry to inform you that your husband, Mr. Allyson, has been murdered. His body was found on the..."

The news hit us like a ton of bricks, and in that moment, everything around us came to a standstill. It was as if time itself had stopped, and the world had gone completely silent.

I couldn't believe what I had just heard. My dad, who had worked so hard to provide for us, was gone. It was like a bad dream, but unfortunately, it was our reality.

My siblings had no idea what was going on, but they could sense the somber mood in the room. My mom sat there with tears streaming down her face, trying to hold back the sobs that threatened to escape her throat. I felt a deep sense of emptiness inside me, like a part of me had been ripped away.

"Where was he found?" mom asked. *"He was found on the ground behind a gas station on Van Dyke and Mack. Would you mind*

coming to the coroner's office to verify the body? We have his wallet with his identification but he doesn't look recognizable. I'm terribly sorry to deliver this news."

My mom screamed out, "I can't! I just can't right now officer." She slammed the phone down and fell to the floor screaming even more. My brothers and I tried to console her.

"What's wrong mommy?" Jeffrey asked twice. She didn't answer him. "Dad's dead." I whispered trying not to make mom feel worse. Both boys began crying and hugging mom. I stood up stunned and felt like my legs were going to collapse from under me. I plopped down on the couch as quickly as I could and let my tears fall in silence.

As the realization set in, my mind raced back to the visitors that had been coming to our house, the dangerous-looking men that my dad had been involved with. Had they finally caught up with him? Was he killed because of his association with them? My mind was

plagued with questions, and I couldn't fathom the thought of never seeing my dad again.

The news of his death brought an end to the little hope we had for a better life. My dad was gone, and with him, our means of survival. We were left with nothing but the memories of a loving father, who did everything he could to provide for us.

CHAPTER TWO

Sins of Survival

Death swept my father away from us during the most critical juncture of our lives, leaving a void that resonated with sorrow throughout our home. As the sole breadwinner, his absence weighed heavily on our shoulders, casting a shadow of financial uncertainty over our future.

My mother valiantly tried to navigate the labyrinth of responsibilities and obligations that came crashing down upon her. She sought refuge in a work-study program, grasping at every opportunity to secure a meager stipend. She felt like that could alleviate the burden of our mounting bills.

The days pressed on, each one a grueling journey. along. How can I forget my father? He had been the thread that bound our family together. His unwavering presence was a source of strength that propelled us forward. His life had been ruthlessly stolen away, leaving us grappling with unanswered questions.

The circumstances surrounding his death remained shrouded in a chilling mystery, a puzzle that refused to yield its secrets.

They found his lifeless body on a notorious street, infamous for its dealings with drug dealers and addicts. Whispers echoed through the neighborhood, claiming that he had been mercilessly strangled. However, amid the fragmented rumors, I overheard my mother's sorrow-laden conversation with my grandmother, where she confessed that he had suffered a more gruesome fate.

"They said that he was shot 3 times. Once in the back of his neck. Once on the side of his face. One in the front of his head." Mom explained crying. Three bullets ended his life in an act of unthinkable violence.

Each day became a battle to resume our lives. We struggled to find a semblance of normalcy amidst the gaping hole left by my father's departure. My mother mustered the strength to pursue her nursing studies. Beneath her facade, it was evident that her heart was shattered and her will to persist was hanging by a thread.

We hoped and yearned for a miracle. We sought solace in the belief that somehow, against all odds, our shattered lives would be made whole again. A suffocating sadness enveloped every aspect of my life.

My mother's once vibrant countenance now carried the weight of sorrow, casting a somber aura around her. Jeffrey suffered a decline in both physical and mental health. His stability slipped away like sand through our fingers. Witnessing his deteriorating condition shattered me. I grappled with the helplessness of our circumstances.

Anger burned within me, fueled by the rapid descent into chaos that our lives had taken. Yet, what gnawed at my sanity even more, was the overwhelming sense of hopelessness that consumed us. We had lost everything, and the future seemed impossibly bleak. To compound our woes, our landlord incessantly threatened us with eviction, a constant reminder of our precarious existence.

One day when my mother went to school, Julian and I found ourselves wandering the streets aimlessly.

We were starving. We had hope that a compassionate stranger might extend a helping hand, offering us a morsel of sustenance. Desperation clouded my thoughts, and at times, I yearned to beg, yearned for others to show us kindness. However, my spirit wavered, unable to summon the courage required for such actions.

The first night my mother failed to return home, I had waited anxiously with my ears strained to catch the familiar sound of her voice. Sometimes, I could hear her greeting our neighbors as she made her way towards our door. This time, all I heard were distant voices carried by the wind and the fading echoes of passing automobiles.

I remained awake throughout the dead of night, worried with fear. The last meal my siblings and I had shared was in the afternoon, and usually, my mother would return with something.. This time, she didn't show up. We were in a state of hunger and uncertainty that pierced our souls.

Images of my father, stolen from us by a cruel fate, flashed through my mind, fueling my anxiety. What if something terrible had happened to my mother too? The uncertainty weighed heavily upon my young shoulders, and my imagination conjured up scenarios that sent shivers down my spine.

It was the following day, around 11 am, when a car pulled up outside our house, bringing my mother safely to our doorstep. The driver was an elderly man with a stooped posture and weathered features. He faded from my memory like an elusive shadow. He was not my concern at the moment.

Relief washed over me at the sight of my mother's return and a surge of joy rushed through my mind. I also had the nagging curiosity of where she had been. She carried bags filled with groceries, and though I was grateful for her safety, I couldn't resist the overwhelming urge to inquire about her absence.

"Mom, why didn't you come home last night?" I asked.
"I was working," she replied, her voice laced with weariness.
Concern etched deep lines on my face as I struggled to
comprehend her response.

Deeply within me, an unease persisted. It was evident that
my mother was burdened by secrets, wrestling with her
own struggles to protect and care for us. Her love for us
burned with an intensity unmatched, and she would go to
great lengths to shield us from harm. Yet, the strain she
carried was a silent testament to the battles she fought
in silence.

The changes in her behavior became increasingly apparent,
leaving me bewildered and uncertain about the path she
was treading. Though there was still food on our table,
her absences grew longer. It turned into two or three-day
spans, particularly on weekends. With my young eyes
taking in every detail, I couldn't help but notice the shift
in her appearance.

Seductive clothing, carefully chosen to accentuate her features, became her daily attire. She adorned herself in garments that were meant to captivate the gaze of men, a deliberate choice to allure and enchant.

It was in the evenings, as dusk settled upon the horizon, that she would transform herself, slipping into garments that did not resemble my mother at all. She would disappear into her room, emerging shortly after as a different person altogether. Her once casual demeanor gave way to an air of allure and mystery. She meticulously applied makeup with precision, her clothes revealed her private parts, and her scent lingered in the air.

The streets became her stage, and the night became her realm. Like a chameleon, she would slip into the shadows, blending seamlessly into the dimly lit corners of the city. It became evident to me that my mother had taken on a new profession. It involved exchanging her time and companionship for money from cruel and reckless men.

During the day, a procession of men would arrive at our doorstep, each one casting a shadow of uncertainty over my young mind. They would drop her off with their fleeting presence leaving behind an unspoken understanding of their intentions. Their visits were transient, leaving me to ponder the nature of their relationship with my mother and the toll it was taking on her spirit.

My mom already made new friends. These were prostitutes who frequent our humble home. Like my mom, they wore seductive clothes, would arrive at our doorstep with a familiarity that suggested a shared bond. They greeted my mother with hugs and laughter, their voices carrying a weight of mischief and secrecy.

At first, I believed these women to be my mother's friends, seeking solace and camaraderie in their shared experiences. They would gather in the living room, their conversations filled with innuendos and whispers that I strained to overhear. It was during these gatherings that I glimpsed the truth that lurked beneath their veneer of friendship.

Their conversations, often punctuated by bursts of raucous laughter, revolved around nights spent in dimly lit bars, secret rendezvous with strangers, and the allure of easy money. They exchanged stories of encounters with powerful individuals and shared tips on how to navigate the treacherous waters of their profession. It became evident that these women, like my mother, were engaged in a world that blurred the lines between friendship, companionship, and the world of the night.

They spoke with a casual nonchalance about their chosen path, as if it were an everyday occurrence. Their shared experiences bonded them together, creating a sisterhood of sorts, where they found solace and understanding in one another's company.

These women became a regular presence in our lives. Their visits grew more frequent, their laughter and camaraderie echoing through the walls of our home. They brought with them a sense of excitement and adventure, but also an undercurrent of danger and unpredictability.

Sometimes, I would sneak out of my room and hide in the shadows, observing their interactions from a safe distance. Their laughter would fill the air as they recounted tales of their escapades, their voices carrying a mixture of pride and resignation. It was in these moments that I began to understand the complexities of their world, the choices they had made, and the sacrifices they endured.

Questions swirled within me, like whispers in a darkened room. Was this a new routine imposed by her nursing school, a requirement that demanded she dress provocatively and mingle with strangers? My instincts told me otherwise. Something didn't add up. My mother, the embodiment of love and sacrifice, had become entangled in a web I couldn't fully understand.

My Father's death affected my mom greatly. Whenever she wasn't engulfed in sorrow, she would seek solace in alcohol or drugs. Evenings became synonymous with her departure, as she slipped out of the house, leaving me yearning for her presence and craving the connection we once shared.

I wanted to tell her many things. I desired her guidance and support. I remember the sinking feeling in my stomach when I discovered my younger brother, Julian, experimenting with the very drugs that had become my mother's refuge. I tried to convey the gravity of the situation, but I still craved my mother's presence as the adult, the one who could enforce the necessary rules and intervene when needed.

The fear that welled up within me was twofold. It wasn't just the fear of my mother's absence, but rather the transformation I witnessed. It was a change that turned her into a stranger. Her once familiar face now bore the marks of a different person, and her actions left me unsettled.

The mother I had known, the pillar of strength and unconditional love, seemed to be slipping away, replaced by a fragmented version who sought solace in prostitution and drugs rather than embracing her role as a caregiver.

One morning, my mother hastily left the house. I heard her voice filled with a sense of urgency. *"Jade, I need you to pack your things and help your brothers pack as well. We're leaving this place."* she instructed. Her words were ringing with a mix of determination and apprehension.

"Where are we going?" I asked curiously. Her response was vague as she made her way out. "Don't worry about that part. Just please do what I asked." The door slammed.

While gathering our belongings, my hands were trembling with both anticipation and anxiety. I stumbled upon a folded piece of paper hidden amidst my mother's personal items. My heart sank as I realized it was her expulsion letter from the nursing school. The weight of the truth bore down on me as I read the words that shattered my image of her.

The accusations were grave: stealing and using prescription drugs on multiple occasions. The tears welled up in my eyes as empathy flooded my soul.

I knew deep down that her addiction and questionable lifestyle were born out of the burdens we, her children, unknowingly placed upon her. The loss of our beloved father and the relentless financial difficulties had slowly chipped away at her spirit, driving her to seek solace in the wrong places.

Mom returned in a weathered truck, its faded paint bearing witness to countless journeys taken. The vehicle belonged to a man I had glimpsed dropping my mother off on numerous occasions. He was a mysterious figure whose presence both intrigued and unsettled me.

He was tall and rugged, he exuded an air of arrogance that seemed at odds with our modest surroundings. His arms were covered with tattoos, each marking a story I could only imagine. He stood there, leaning against the truck as a silent observer of our unfolding reality.

I approached him cautiously with my heart pounding in my chest. *"You... you're one of my mother's clients, aren't you?"* I managed to utter with a mix of curiosity and trepidation.

He nodded, and his gaze met mine with a hint of remorse. *"Yeah, kid, that's right,"* he replied with his voice carrying a weight of acknowledgment. *"Your mom reached out to me, and said she needed help."*

A surge of conflicting emotions washed over me. I grappled with the understanding that my mother had gone to great lengths, perhaps even compromising herself, to secure his assistance. The realization left me with a bitter taste in my mouth.

Together, we loaded our belongings onto the truck, I could see that Jeffrey and Julian were confused at how fast our lives were changing. They huddled close and their small frames were dwarfed by the truck's worn-out seats. Their wide eyes darted around, seeking reassurance amidst the chaos that had consumed our family.

As the engine of the car roared, I could feel the vibrations echoed through my trembling heart.

I turned my gaze towards the house for the last time. My eyes traced the familiar contours of the walls that had witnessed our joys and sorrows. Memories flooded my heart, carrying me back to the days when my dad would enter with joy, calling out to us.

I could almost hear the echoes of my younger brothers' p ayful laughter, reverberating through the open spaces that once embraced us. There, amidst it all, was my mother, a pillar of unwavering love and solace.

Looking at my mother now, all I could see was a defeated and broken woman. The weight of reality pressed upon my chest, leaving me breathless in its wake. The mother I once knew, vibrant and resilient, now stood before me as a defeated stranger with her spirit worn down by the trials of life. My brothers, once full of curiosity and dreams, now appeared lost and their innocence was overshadowed by the overwhelming loneliness that surrounded us.

A pang of helplessness pierced my soul as I witnessed the flickering flames of hope gradually waning in their eyes.

Warm tears cascaded down my cheeks, tracing a path of sorrow and longing. Each droplet carried with it the weight of our shattered dreams and the anguish of leaving behind the only sanctuary we had ever known.

As I looked at my mother, her own tears silently betraying the immense pain she carried within, I realized that we were not just leaving a physical place, but bidding farewell to the sanctuary of love, comfort, and familiarity that had enveloped us. The world beyond those doors loomed before us, veiled in a shroud of uncertainty, its countless challenges and trials stretching out like an endless abyss.

"Mom, where are we going? What's really going on?"
I asked. Before my mother could get a word out,
the strange man interrupted her. *"What's going on is none of your business little lady. You must learn how to stay in a child's place."*

Ignoring him as intentionally as I could,
I spoke with more confidence and louder, "Mom!"
She turned her head to look at me,

our eyes met and I wanted it to be a caring moment as we had shared many times before. Instead, she put her index finger on her lips and said, "Shhhhhh."

CHAPTER THREE

The Unveiling of Darkness

Our family was constantly on the move now. We wouldn't settle down in one place for long. We hopped from one place to another, often finding ourselves in smaller and less welcoming environments. It was a challenging and uncertain time for us, especially after the loss of my father. However, amidst the turbulence, there was one man who unexpectedly became an integral part of our lives.

His name was Kingsley.

Remember when my mom first made the decision to start our lives anew in a different neighborhood? Kingsley was the stranger who assisted us with our relocation.

Little did I know then that he played a pivotal role in helping my mom secure the apartment that we moved into after leaving Detroit.

While my mother slept with many men for money and kept different fleeting relationships, there were few individuals who left

an indelible mark on my perception of my childhood, and Kingsley became one of them.

Kingsley and my mom started a romantic relationship. He made promises to fill the void left by my dad and vowed to take care of us in every possible way. Having been married twice before and having two children from those marriages, Kingsley carried his own complex life experiences.

Although I never had the chance to meet his previous family members, my mom assured me that they would visit us one day. Nonetheless, it was Kingsley's presence and actions that held the most impact on my young life.

At first, Kingsley was a questionable man in my mind. However, he became extremely kind. His contagious smile lit up the room, and his towering presence and broad shoulders gave me a much- needed sense of security. He became a frequent visitor, arriving with thoughtful gifts and bags of groceries. The sunlight of my mother's smile, which had been dimmed since my father's passing,

began to slowly return, and hope blossomed within our little family once again.

It seemed as though he was the missing piece to our struggling family, but it became evident later that his presence in our lives was not a blessing but a curse in disguise. The way he changed was astonishing, as if a switch had been flipped, revealing a sinister side I had never anticipated.

It was clear that he harbored a deep resentment towards us, exploiting our vulnerability in the face of grief and poverty as a means to manipulate and control. The sly predator within him preyed upon our desperation, using it as a tool to maintain his twisted hold over our lives.

Everyday, the sadness in our home became unbearable, accompanied by the regular screams that echoed through the walls from my mother. The sounds of my mother's agonizing pain filled the air as she was being abused by the monstrous man.

I can remember waking up in the middle of the night one time to my mother screaming, *"I didn't yell at you! I was trying to explain..."* *"There's nothing for you to explain to me. If I say do it or don't do it, that's what I mean. You don't ever talk back to me, understand?"*

Fear consumed me while I heard my mom crying uncontrollably yelling okay from time to time. That's when I realized that Kingsley was hitting her. It was during these moments that the true nature of his malevolence emerged, revealing his insatiable desire to violate my mother both physically and sexually.

To him, her body was nothing more than an object to claim, regardless of her lack of consent or the emotional scars it left behind. I could tell that the wounds mom bore were not just physical; her sense of worth was degraded and her spirit broken.

On many occasions, I would walk in to meet my mom lying broken and violated on the cold floor. She would be clenching her knees to her chest, rocking and crying. *"Jade, don't worry about me. Just*

go away, okay?" Those words became repetitive in our home more times than not.

Despite his fading promises of love, Kingsley showed no hesitation in subjecting her to the most brutish forms of abuse. Behind closed doors, he reveled in the torment he inflicted upon my mother, relishing in the power and control he wielded over her.

The bond we had hoped would provide solace and support, transformed into a suffocating nightmare, a web of manipulation and pain from which we struggled to escape. As a witness to her suffering, my heart bled with helplessness and anger.

Kingsly had many friends who came around our house too, they were cut from the same cloth, bad birds that flock together, amplifying the malevolence that radiated from their collective presence. Nights at our house were no longer filled with the warm glow of family bonding or the comforting sounds of laughter.

Instead, they transformed into a den of debauchery, fueled by alcohol and reckless indulgence. Kingsley and his cohorts would drink to excess, their raucous laughter and slurred speech piercing through the stillness of the night.

Their female companions, or rather, the prostitutes they brought with them, were no better. They were a part of the obscured underbelly that thrived within this corrupt circle. These women, shrouded in a haze of despair, were reduced to objects of temporary sexual pleasure and they knew it.

My mother, being helpless, made a decision for the sake of my younger siblings. Jeffrey, burdened by his own demons, was placed in a cheap psychiatric center, a place that offered the faint promise of healing. Julian, too young to comprehend the confusions unfolding around him, found refuge in the house of our grandparents.

As for me, I remained by my mother's side, shedding a piece of my childhood innocence, trading the joys of youth for the

responsibilities that were thrust upon me. Birthdays, for me, were a mere reminder of what was lost. While other children cherished the excitement of presents, cakes, candles, and treats, mine consisted of adult burdens that demanded my attention.

My mother even loaned me out to one of her friends who had a clothing business. This opportunity came to fruition through the friend expressing the need for help. She told my mom that she would teach me a trade after school in exchange for my dedicated service. This would also keep me out of the house while Kingsley had his frequent visitors.

The arrangement was far from glamorous. My days were filled with a myriad of tasks that extended beyond clothing. I became the jack- of-all-trades so to speak, embracing roles that ranged from cleaning and organizing to running various errands. It was a demanding routine, one that required both physical and mental endurance. As if school wasn't already enough.

My assistance was beyond the store. As my boss became more acquainted with my help, she entrusted me with additional responsibilities that spilled over into her personal life. I would find myself frequenting her house, becoming intimately familiar with its layout. I would dust and polish furniture, scrub floors, and perform a host of other chores that ensured her home was kept in pristine condition.

With all these things, when I got home in the evenings, the toxic presence of Kingsley's friends persisted. They would stumble into our home, disheveled and disoriented, accompanied by their prostitutes who clung to them like shadows.

The aftermath of their reckless revelry was a scene of devastation, an unholy collage of shattered glass, cigarette butts, ashes, and the unmistakable evidence of their depravity. Used condoms were strewn about as reminders of their base desires.

As dawn broke, and the last remnants of their presence dissipated, I would face the arduous task of cleaning up the house. Armed with a broom and a heavy heart, I would sweep away the debris.

My young mind struggled to grasp the perplexing transformation my mother underwent, morphing from the gentle, innocent woman I had known into a prostitute entangled in the clutches of drug and substance addiction. It was as if a veil had been torn away, exposing a side of her I had never fathomed.

To compound matters, Kingsly, unashamedly, displayed his contempt for our existence. In his eyes, my mother was a mere object of pleasure, subservient to his every whim without a trace of inquiry. Often, I found myself a powerless witness, forced to observe the cruel grip with which he handled my dear mother.

There were countless instances where I could only watch in helplessness as he manhandled her. His hands were leaving bruises and scars she would bear for the rest of her life. The air in our home

was thick with tension, suffocating under the weight of their toxic dynamic.

As time stretched its weary limbs, these unsettling moments became the order of the day in our house. One day, he came home with two of his friends, and from their gaunt frames, hollow eyes, and tattered appearance, one could tell that they had long lost their way, consumed by their own flaws.

A heated argument started when he said he has given his friends permission to sleep with my mother. My mother, summoning the remnants of her strength, vehemently rejected Kingsley's proposition. *"Kingsley, it's already late. Do I really have to do this?"*

In a display of rage and entitlement, he unleashed a searing slap across her face, the sound reverberating through the air. The impact left her stunned and vulnerable, her spirit momentarily shattered. *"What did I tell you about talking back huh? Do what I said before*

I get in that flat ass of yours! You should be glad that anybody wants you anyway."

My mom had had enough I think because their words clashed like thunderbolts. They were fierce and unforgiving. Kingsly's voice, laced with venom, pierced the room as he hurled insults at my mother. The weight of his accusations stung in my ears. *"You ungrateful bitch!"* he spat, his words dripping with contempt.

Unable to bear witness to my mother's dishonor in person, my pulse quickened as I went to the front room with boldness. Kingsly stood tall above me, flanked by his two friends. Their sunken eyes held a hint of sickness, their appearances mirroring the turmoil within.

I remember how my frail little limbs were shivering as I pieced together Kingsly's intentions. He brazenly repeated that he had granted his friends permission to sleep with my mom, and their eyes were gleaming with sinister desire. The room seemed to shrink, suffocating under the weight of his perverse proposition.

I mustered whatever courage I had left and with fragile determination, I approached Kingsley, tugging at his shirt in a desperate attempt to pull him away from my mom. The violent force within him quickly turned his gaze towards me, launching a vicious kick that sent me crashing into a corner.

"Back up off of me Jade. I swear you don't want me to handle you like I handle your mama!"

From the helpless corner, I could only watch in horror as my mother became a victim to the wickedness that surrounded her. These vile men, driven by their own depravity, descended upon her like ravenous beasts, taking what they believed was their entitlement. My heart shattered as her cries echoed through the room, a haunting sound to the violation unfolding before my tear- filled eyes.

Through the anguish, she cried, muffled by the violence inflicted upon her. It was a scene that assaulted my senses. How could the world be so cruel? My heart sank in helplessness as I bore witness

to an unforgettable moment. My beloved mother was defiled and gang-raped by these three wicked men who took their turn to have their lustful feel.

Kingsley turned to me, sitting stunned on the floor and said, *"Go to your room girl. Get a little older and you'll get your turn to make me my money too."*

What did he just say to me? Did he say what I think he said? Instead of dwelling on his evil words, I took what felt like my only chance to run and did just that.

The last day I saw Kingsly, I was in the clothing store going about my routine when my boss informed me that there was an emergency at home and I needed to go home immediately. My heart skipped a beat as worry crept into my mind. Without wasting a second, I hurriedly made my way back, my footsteps filled with a sense of foreboding.

As I approached our house, my eyes widened with disbelief. A police car stood parked in front of our yard, its presence casting an air of authority and concern. A crowd of concerned neighbors had gathered, their anxious whispers punctuating the air. I pushed my way through the gathering with my heart pounding in my chest.

Inside our house was scattered, an obvious indication of the violence that had transpired. The walls seemed to whisper tales of unspeakable violations I could only imagine, while the air was heavy with tension. My eyes searched frantically for my mother, and finally, I found her lying on the couch.

Her face was pale and bruised, her body wrapped in a shroud of pain. She had been brutally attacked by Kingsley, but this time, it was different as she struggled to hold on to her life.

The police informed me that Kingsly had not only physically assaulted my mother but had also poured acid on her. The very thought made me quiver, and I could hardly comprehend the depths and gravity of the incident. My mother's condition was critical.

They told me that her life was hanging by a thread. I have never been more scared in my life as I saw her being rushed to the hospital in a desperate bid to save her.

This was not the first time Kingsly had attempted to kill her. Memories flooded back, vivid and haunting, of the previous instances of abuse and cruelty. I recalled how he had callously pushed her down the little steps at the entrance of our house, leaving her battered and broken. And on some nights, he would lock her out, leaving her vulnerable and exposed to the darkness.

I was ecstatic that the police had Kingsley in custody and heartbroken that my mother was in horrific shape. How in the world could she let things get so out of control. My dad would have never had the nerve or heart to hurt us like this.

CHAPTER FOUR

AT THE COUNTRYSIDE

Fortunately, my mom was able to recover from her injuries. Barely having left the confines of the hospital, she made a heartfelt decision that would shape the course of my journey. Recognizing the weighty burden that figuring out her own life posed, she agreed that I should join my brother, Julian, at our grandmother's place.

Nestled in the countryside, their humble abode beckoned as a place of solace and support. It was a realm where my mother believed I could find respite, and where her own burdens might be lightened.

Visits to my grandparents had been rare occasions in the past, limited to only two cherished trips with my father. Each journey was an adventure that inscribed its essence into the deepest recesses of my young mind. The memories of those fleeting experiences remained. It was a world unlike any other, where every moment was filled with awe-inspiring discoveries.

I can still vividly recall the first time we arrived at my grandparents' countryside home. As the car rolled to a stop along the gravel driveway, I flung open the door, my senses immediately overwhelmed by the scents that danced upon the breeze. The fragrance of freshly cut grass mingled with the sweet perfume of blooming flowers, saturating the air with a delightful bouquet that awakened my spirit.

My grandmother, a gentle soul with eyes that sparkled like morning dew, greeted us with open arms and a warm smile. "Welcome, my dear," she exclaimed, her voice laced with genuine delight. I embraced her tightly, feeling the love and tenderness that radiated from her. The wrinkles on her face told stories of a life well-lived, and in her presence, I found solace and comfort.

The sprawling vista that greeted me were like living paintings, a blend of emerald meadows stretching as far as the eye could see, adorned with golden wildflowers that swayed in harmony with the

gentle breeze. My father stood beside me, his face reflecting a shared appreciation for the beauty that surrounded us.

"Look, my dear," my father pointed towards the distant hills, their peaks kissed by the golden rays of the setting sun. *"These lands have witnessed countless seasons, and witnessed the flow of life. It's a place of peace and serenity. A world where time slows down, and nature embraces you with open arms."*

I could still remember how on the following day we went on a long walk through the serene wood. While resting beneath the shade of a towering oak tree, my father's eyes twinkled with warmth.

"Do you see that bird, perched up high on that branch?" he asked, pointing toward a vibrant blue jay that sang its melodious song. *"It's said that their songs carry the hopes and dreams of those who listen. What do you hear?"* I closed my eyes, allowing the sweet melodies to wash over me. Images of distant lands flooded my mind. *"I hear a world filled with adventure,"* I replied with a smile playing upon my lips.

Unlike the city I was accustomed to, the countryside breathed with its own rhythm, its residents predominantly farmers who seemed immune to the anxieties and desperation that plagued the modern world. They were custodians of the earth, their hands bearing the calluses of hard work, and their spirits carrying the wisdom of generations intertwined with the cycles of the seasons.

I didn't get to know my grandfather well during those visits. Our encounter was a fleeting moment that left me with more questions than answers. I caught a mere glimpse of him though, a man in his seventies, yet he seemed to defy the passage of time. Despite the visible signs of aging evident on his weathered face, there was a surprising vitality within him.

He had spent his life working for the man as he would say. He achieved a level of success that garnered respect from those who knew him. Although his body bore the weight of years, he retained a certain youthful vigor in his stature, standing tall with a hint of the strength that had carried him through a lifetime of labor.

His baritone voice commanded attention, suggesting a natural authority that had once held sway over others.

There was also a sternness to his presence, a lingering suggestion of a disciplinarian nature. The lines on his face spoke of a life lived without compromise, carved by the hardships and challenges he had faced along the way. Though our encounter was brief, his demeanor conveyed a sense of seriousness, as if he carried the weight of regrets within him.

However, I had a special bond with my grandmother, a connection that transcended words and touched the depths of my soul. Her presence in my life provided a refuge from the toxicity that often surrounded me. In a world of negativity, my grandmother emanated a different kind of warmth and love, one that remains unparalleled even to this day.

My grandmother exuded a sense of contentment and gratitude for what she had. It was as if she possessed a secret treasure, hidden within her heart, that allowed her to find joy in the simplest of

things. Her resilience and ability to find happiness in the face of adversity left an indelible mark on my young mind.

Deeply devoted to her Christian faith, my grandmother instilled in me the importance of spirituality and a connection with God. During those two occasions spent with her, I can recall the earnestness in her voice as she emphasized the significance of my father drawing closer to God. It was not merely a passing remark but a heartfelt plea, driven by her unwavering belief in the power of faith to guide and protect us.

Having the opportunity to stay with my grandparents held a ray of hope in my heart, a chance to escape the suffocating toxicity of the city that had become my daily reality. With anticipation coursing through my veins, I gathered my meager belongings, carefully tucking them into a small, worn bag.

Among my possessions, the most cherished item was a simple gown, a gift from my father, which I clung to despite its undersized nature. Its frayed edges and faded colors carried a weight of

sentimental value, a tangible reminder of the love
I shared with him.

The morning was charged with a sense of urgency as I scurried behind my determined mother, both of us driven by a shared determination to catch the bus that would transport us to the countryside. It was a journey filled with weariness and excitement, the long ride gradually taking its toll on our tired bodies. Yet, amidst the fatigue, there were moments when my mind wandered, entranced by the passing scenery that unfolded outside the window.

As the bus traversed the winding roads, I enjoyed the beauty of nature that played out before my eyes. The trees stood tall and proud, their leaves swaying in sync with the gentle breeze, as if beckoning me towards a world untouched by the hardships of city life. Rolling hills adorned the horizon, their undulating contours painting a picturesque backdrop against the sky. It was a sight that breathed life into my weary soul.

Lost between moments of drifting into sleep and getting lost in my own thoughts, I found respite in the journey itself. The bus seemed to glide effortlessly through the wind, carrying me away from the noise and chaos of the world I was leaving behind. With each passing mile, the weight of my worries began to lift, replaced by a growing sense of anticipation for the new chapter that awaited me in the countryside.

I stared out the window and the swaying of the bus lulled me into a state of tranquility. As the bus pressed on, I hoped and prayed it was going to be for good. I knew that I was inching closer to a new beginning.

My mother and I didn't really speak to each other much during this ride. I believe that she needed this ride to rid her of her stress and anxiety that our city lent her. I am surprised and thankful that she survived what I thought was truly the end of her life. I could only imagine what her thoughts could be. Although I hated leaving my mother behind, alone to pick up the broken pieces of her life, I was

relieved that I could have my own fresh start.
Was that horrible of me? Selfish? Maybe a little.

Our bus came to a halt at the village's bus stop, my mother
and I disembarked, greeted by a sense of uncertainty.
The bus ride had been long and tiring. The bustling city had
gradually faded into the distance. Luck seemed to smile
upon us as we found ourselves in the right place at the
right time.

As we continued to rattle along the dusty road, revealing a
somber tableau of hardship and struggle. The once
enchanting facade dissolved before me. Poverty and neglect
cast a gloomy shadow over the place, with the weight of
despair on the faces of those who called this place home.

The country, even seemed, to become a battleground for
vices that stained its once pristine reputation.
Drug addiction, alcoholism, and prostitution lurked in the
corners, haunting the lives of its inhabitants like specters
of darkness.

Unlike the bustling streets of the city, where cars and automobiles painted the scene, in the countryside, such luxuries were rare occurrences. The sight of a passing truck, while uncommon, held a glimmer of fortune. During our travels my mother and I found ourselves faced with residents from the country fixating upon us. .

Their eyes bore witness to our shared struggles, as if they could discern the weight of our journey and the tragedies we sought to escape as we traveled deeper into the heart of the country. .

When we arrived at my grandparents' house, my eyes quickly found grandma standing eagerly outside, her face lighting up with joy and anticipation. It was evident that she had been anxiously awaiting our arrival. I had a burst of excitement. I jumped off the truck and rushed into her open arms, feeling an overwhelming sense of love and belonging envelop me.

In that moment, all worries and uncertainties faded away, replaced by the purest form of affection I had ever experienced. Her embrace

was heavenly. It was a place where I felt cherished and desired, a feeling that had eluded me throughout my young life.

"Well hello ladies! It's so good to see you two!" Grandma said as she went to hug my mom. *"You too grandma!.* I exclaimed. My mom hugged her and said, *"Thank you so much for this. I don't know what I would do without you stepping in. I know that it's probably inconvenient..."* Grandma stopped her, *"Now, you know that my grandchildren are no inconvenience. I just wished that you would have sent Jade sooner."*

My mom nodded and looked down as she didn't want us to see the tears that were building in her eyes. Though my grandfather was absent that evening, the presence of Uncle P and Michelle filled the house with a sense of familiarity. Uncle P was in his late 30s or early 40s.

He greeted us warmly, his face lined with a genuine smile. Michelle was uncle P's daughter around 14 years old. Her energy and enthusiasm were contagious, bringing a vibrant energy to the

humble abode. She was there to spend the night with me to show me around and give me a friend to talk to for the first few days.

We all sat around shooting the breeze as grandma finished up her dinner. I was also happy to see my brother who grabbed mom so hard and hugged her so tight that I thought she was going to break in two. *"I missed you mom. You too Jade."* He said as he punched me playfully in my shoulder.

When grandpa appeared, I struggled to recognize him at first. He was wearing a worn but unwashed shirt and faded shorts. His feet carried him swiftly towards us. Despite his appearance, I couldn't help but feel an immense rush of joy as I embraced him tightly.

However, I couldn't help but notice a faint scent of something burnt lingering in the air around him. *"It's good to see y'all. Let me go and change out of this work clothes."* He replied as he walked towards their bedroom.

Grandma stepped out and said, "Jade, let me show you your room. Julian, get her things." The small room that I was given was a space that resembled more of a storage area than a proper bedroom. The house itself lacked a lot of space. It only had three bedrooms. One belonging to my grandparents, another to my brother and the other for me.

The enticing aroma of Grandma's cooking filled the air. The kitchen became a hub of bustling activity as she skillfully prepared a hearty meal for us all. However, the harmonious atmosphere shattered when the sound of heavy footsteps and laughter echoed through the house.

Grandpa had returned with his unmistakable signs of intoxication, loud demeanor, and an unkempt aura that seemed to precede him like a dark cloud. This, I would soon come to realize, was his trademark, an unfortunate habit.

As he stumbled towards the couch, a noticeable shift occurred within our small gathering. Feeling the weight of uncertainty and

confusion settle upon me, I glanced at Julian searching for guidance amidst the gloom that had suddenly enveloped us. Recognizing the need to make sense of the unsettling situation, I followed Julian as he led me away from the discord that swirled around us.

When dinner was ready, we came together around their long rectangular table and became partakers of the delicious food that grandma prepared. *"Everything is so delicious mom."* My mom said while she was eating the chicken breast that was delightfully crispy and flaky. *"She's the best cook in town."* Grandpa spoke after taking a drink from his beer bottle that grandma had given him with his plate.

Conversation continued as we all just got caught up with things that had been happening. Mom didn't mention anything about her and Kingsley. I was grateful for that because I just wanted to forget about him as quickly as possible. *"So, you're moving in with us too huh?"* Grandpa asked, looking at me. *" Yes I am if it's okay grandpa?"*

"It's a little too late for you to ask me now. Your mama should've asked before bringing you all the way down here. I guess we're officially the daycare center now." Appalled by his rude response, I laughed, "Grandpa, you're silly. I know that you are glad for us to be here." "Yes we are sweetie. Don't you mind your grandfather, he thinks that he's a comedian around here." Grandma spoke with the intent to clean up his comment.

"Thank you so much dad. I promise you that they won't be here long. I just need a little time to get things situated back home, okay?" Mom assured him. "Unh huh." He grumbled back. As the night wore on, and the echoes of Grandpa's disturbance subsided, a quiet stillness settled upon the house.

That night, something strange happened. An eerie stillness hung in the air, broken only by the soft rustle of bedsheets and the distant chirping of nocturnal creatures. I found myself stirred from the depths of my sleep, my senses alert and attuned to the unfamiliar presence that permeated the room. Blinking away the remnants of sleep, I peered into the darkness, my eyes drawn to a haunting sight.

There, on the edge of the mat, sat Michelle, her figure hunched in a posture of anguish. Her bowed head concealed her face, veiling the worries that consumed her. I watched in silence, intrigued and concerned. The allure of returning to a much-needed rest after the day's exhaustion tugged at my weary mind, yet the mystery surrounding Michelle's midnight vigil held me captive.

As I strained to comprehend the enigma unfolding before me, a faint sound reached my ears. It was the delicate sounds of stifled sobs. I looked to see Michelle's tears flowing, her anguish kept in check, but her pain palpable nonetheless.

Crawling toward her, I reached out to touch her trembling shoulder, but a surge of resistance met my touch. She recoiled, wrenching her head upward to meet my gaze for the first time. Her once lustrous hair now tangled and unruly, her eyes reddened and swollen from tears.

She averted her gaze, unwilling to meet my inquisitive stare, as if shielding herself from the vulnerability of her pain. Her sorrow hung heavy in the air. In that moment, she turned away, her tears continuing to cascade in a silence. I felt a pang of helplessness, unsure of how to comfort her or ease the burdens that weighed upon her shoulders.

In the stillness of that night, I became acutely aware of the complexities that resided within the souls of those around me, vaults of untold stories, concealed pain, and unspoken struggles. My heart began to feel heavy as I retreated back to my own corner of the room. The hushed whispers of the night accompanied her tears.

Awake and plagued by bewilderment, I remained motionless. The girl I had encountered earlier in the evening exuded a radiant aura, her demeanor graceful and serene. Yet now, she appeared lost, fractured, and consumed by a sadness that clung to her like a shroud.

Time seemed to stretch as I watched Michelle's tears flow unabated, their silent cascade echoing the depth of her pain. Thirty long minutes passed, each moment difficult, until finally, exhaustion overtook her trembling form. She laid herself upon the sleeping bag with her tear-stained cheeks still glistening under the soft moonlight that filtered through the window.

The night settled into a serene calm once more. I vowed to seek answers and understanding from my mother who was fast asleep on the couch the next day. As I lay there, contemplating the mysteries that veiled Michelle's pain, a gentle resolve took root within me. I yearned to unravel her story, to offer a listening ear and a compassionate heart. With the dawn on the horizon, I awaited the arrival of a new day.

I was so tired that I soon fell asleep again. When I woke up, the day had fully broken and the street had taken on a different look. People were rushing off to their places of work. I looked for my mom, but grandma told me that she was gone. My heart sank. It felt like a piece of me was gone. I had never really been separated from her

before, but this time, it felt like she wouldn't be coming back for a long time.

"She didn't say goodbye to me." I whispered. I could see Julian, sadly seated on the bench just outside the house. I knew he too had not expected that mom would leave us so soon, and was sad that he couldn't spend more time with her. I went over to him and sat down. We didn't say anything for a long time. We just sat there, watching the people go by.

CHAPTER FIVE

PLUCKED AND PLUNDERED

Deep within me lies this chapter of my life that I have guarded with utmost fear, hesitant to unfurl its raw pages to the world. Silently, I have carried the weight of this untold story throughout the passages of my adult existence. It started when I found myself entrusted to the care of my grandparents.

Within those weathered walls, a reality took root, engraving into my very essence. It was the immutable truth that our lives are not always governed by the reins of control we desperately clutch.

Before then, my childhood was already woven with threads of adversity, interlaced with the loss that tore through our family. In the cruel grip of fate, my father's life was viciously extinguished at the precise moment our yearning for his guidance was most acute. Then I had to witness the unspeakable horrors wrought by the hands of wicked men, leaving indelible scars upon my mom's spirit.

She was violated often, dimming the innocence I had held dear. The flames of anguish burned with a ferocity that surpassed the scorching fires of Hell itself, consuming my senses with an inferno of unimaginable magnitude.

At my grandparents, a disquieting dissonance hung in the air whenever Michelle found herself in the presence of our grandfather. Something I did not understand until later. It was as if an invisible veil of unease draped over her. While grandpa was rarely at home during work, his appearances brought with them an obvious sense of discomfort.

His daily routine painted a picture of a man on the move, his time divided between the toils of his job in the early hours, and the haze of drinking and smoking during twilight hours. Often, he would return home under the cloak of night, long after we had surrendered ourselves to the embrace of sleep. It was in these infrequent encounters that I first perceived the irregularities that set my senses ablaze.

Michelle, in her tender awkwardness, would become restless whenever my grandfather was around. Her movements became unsteady, her coordination faltered, as though she were navigating an unfamiliar terrain. There was an undeniable tension that clung to her demeanor, an invisible weight that burdened her spirit in the presence of grandpa.

As I continue to observe grandfather, a disconcerting realization crept upon me. There was something suspicious about him. It was in the depths of his gaze that the true nature of his intentions revealed itself to me.

His lustful stirs were like the predatory gleam of a hunter closing in on its prey. I felt the primal instinct of self-preservation surge within me, an innate understanding that I stood within the pouncing range, the perilous reach of a merciless predator.

Though my innocence shielded me from fully comprehending his intentions, the unspoken language of fear spoke volumes. It was a

voiceless warning upon my soul, urging me to be cautious, to guard myself against the unseen dangers lurking beneath his seemingly benign facade.

On one fateful day, the narrative of my life took a different and difficult turn, plunging me into a harrowing realm of distress and trauma. The hours weighed heavily upon me as I was home alone. Grandma had gone to the grocery store to get some things for dinner. Julian was out playing with his friend and Michelle was gone. Little did I know that the peace of the empty house would soon be shattered by an encounter that would forever haunt my memories.

As dusk settled, a sense of anticipation clung to the atmosphere. The weary day wore on, and I yearned for the return of grandma. Then, like an unwelcome specter, our grandfather made his way back home.

In my naivety, I believed he had come only to retrieve an item or refresh himself with a quick shower, adhering to his customary

routine. However, destiny had scripted a different narrative, one that would unravel before me in the cruelest of ways.

Minutes passed in silence, disturbed only by the sounds of my own footsteps. It was then that my grandfather called me, his voice had an unsettling undertone. He requested that I prepare hot water for his bath. Obliging his demand, I diligently readied the steaming liquid, its warmth a stark contrast to the cold shiver of apprehension that coursed through my veins.

I approached his room, unaware of the treacherous path upon which I unwittingly trod. Our grandfather, still clad in his tattered work pants, stood before me, his bare torso revealed his strength and ruggedness. A faded towel hung loosely around his weathered neck, a tenuous barrier between his intentions and my innocence.

The weight of the situation pressed upon me an understanding of what lurked within his gaze. His presence loomed over me, casting a shadow upon my tender soul, a silhouette of dominance that threatened to engulf my very being.

His eyes, like two pools of doom, glimmered with a menacing intensity, burdened with secrets, hiding a treacherous venom that only awaited the opportune moment to strike. His calculated calmness veiled his true intentions. He beckoned me to step into his room with his desperate voice disguised as composure.

I approached with cautious steps, it never occurred to me the sheer magnitude of his cravings, for he was, after all, my grandfather. The rumors that circulated, painting him in an unfavorable light, seemed nothing more than whispers in the wind, unverified and dismissed as mere hearsay.

He gestured for me to join him on the bed, an invitation robed in the guise of familial bonding. I obliged, my body tense, perching at the edge as if maintaining a physical distance could shield me from the impending turmoil.

However, as he drew nearer, an acrid scent was in the air, mingling with the heat of his presence. The stale odor of his sweat clung to

my senses, a pungent reminder of the physicality that embodied his being.

The space between us diminished, and his right hand encircled my shoulders, tightening its grip with an unsettling familiarity. I sat there, perched at the precipice of innocence, his presence pressed against me, suffocating my spirit, as his intent seeped into my consciousness like a toxic elixir.

"How old are you, Jade?" he inquired, his words carrying a hint of forced ignorance that seemed out of place. The question itself was strange, for he was well aware of my age. I hesitated for a moment, unsure of how to respond. *"I am twelve years old sir,"* I finally replied.

His response dripped with insincerity, as if feigning surprise at my age. *"Twelve? You do not look twelve at all,"* he remarked. It was a sentiment shared by others I had encountered, as my youthful appearance often belied my true years. Yet, his words carried a

deeper meaning, implying a connection between my age and grownups.

The conversation took an unsettling turn as he probed further, with his hands reaching under my cloth to touch my breast, that made my skin crawl. *"So, you do not have a boyfriend in the city?"* he inquired. I shook my head. *"Why? Have you done it before?"* he persisted. The room seemed to close in around me, trapping me in a claustrophobic web spun by his manipulative words.

Desperation colored his voice as he continued, *"Tell me anything you want, I will do it for you."* It was a hollow promise, one encrusted in false generosity, but it carried with it an air of manipulation. His hand, once resting upon my shoulder, slithered its way further beneath the fabric of my clothing, exploring other parts of my body.

The rough texture of his touch burned against my skin, panic surged within me, urging me to break free from his grasp. I tried to pull away, but his grip tightened, a firm restraint that held me

captive against my will. His voice, though strained, remained calm as he spoke with false paternal concern. *"My child, Papa can take care of you, you know!"*

In that moment, the boundaries crumbled, leaving me trapped in a web of deceit and vulnerability. The realization that the one who should have protected me was now the predator that haunted my nightmares forever scarred my heart. I hoped for escape, for release from his inordinate desires. I began to shiver as I remembered my mom's piercing cries when she was abused by wicked men.

I attempted to free myself from his hold, instinctively pulling away with all of my might. However, his grip remained unyielding, his strong hands firmly clamping down on my wrist like an iron vice. The realization struck me like a bolt of lightning. This was far more grave than I had imagined.

I began to tremble uncontrollably. Tears streamed down my face, drenching my clothes. His reassurances, disguised as a plea for calmness, rang in my ears. *"Stay calm, Jade, I won't hurt you,"* he

whispered. His words dripped with a chilling blend of false comfort and malicious intent. It was a warning designed to strip me of any defiance.

"Do what I say, and you will like it," he added. His voice now carried an unsettling mix of authority and sadistic satisfaction. The full weight of his dominance pressed against me, leaving me powerless. I summoned every ounce of strength within my young, trembling frame to challenge his grasp, but my efforts felt feeble and futile against the force of his hold.

Each attempt to wrestle my hands from his grip met with immediate resistance, further reinforcing the inescapable truth. I was trapped at the mercy of a predator disguised as my grandfather. My helplessness grew, overshadowing my fleeting hopes of escape.

It was like I was in a swirling vortex when he sensed that he was not getting what he wanted easily. He violently hurled me onto his bed, its mattress an accomplice to the impending nightmare. A monster now towered above me. Feeble attempts at resistance

materialized as trembling hands pushing against the weight of his loathsome presence.

My body was met with a chilling retribution, as the force of his blows collided with my tender cheek, unleashing such pain that resounded through my skull. As his savage slaps landed on my face, I could only see stars and darkness.

Through tear-streaked eyes, I struggled to maintain a shred of clarity amidst the haze of my tormented consciousness. The world presented itself as a distorted apparition. The man looming over me is consumed by his insatiable desires. He was relentless.

A relentless force hell-bent on claiming what he believed to be his twisted entitlement. In my helplessness, I lay exposed beneath his calloused touch, my garments torn asunder, a painful violation of my very essence.

Then came the moment, a collision of agony and intrusion that forever seared its wretched mark upon my innocence. As he

inserted his manhood into my private part, his thrust was an act of merciless violence. It was like an arrow of torment piercing through the delicate skin. I screamed in protest as he plunged into the sanctity of my virginity.

In that heart-wrenching instant, I felt the essence of my purity shattered. My world torn by a predator who reveled in my suffering. A cry of anguish tore its way through my throat, escaping into the air like a wounded creature's final lament. It was a cry that encapsulated the snapping of my very existence, a raw outpouring of agony that defied description.

My anguished cry was abruptly silenced, suffocated by the cruel hand that clamped over my quivering mouth. His fingers, gnarled and calloused, stifled my voice, robbing me of any semblance of protest or release. Then using his other hand, he pressed me forcefully against the bed, my body yielding to his brute strength.

the stains of his wickedness. I felt betrayed, for the guardian of my safety had become my tormentor. Above all, I felt used, reduced to a vessel for his sick desires.

A tempest of revulsion raged within me, threatening to consume the fragile remains of my shattered self. I yearned for the elusive power to exact my vengeance, to strike back with a force that could obliterate the desecration he had wrought upon my soul. But his commanding voice pierced through my seething rage, tearing me away from the depths of my fury.

"Do not just lie there," his words dripped with contempt, casting a damning shadow over my violated form. The weight of his command propelled me to my feet, but with each step, the evidence of his brutality became starkly visible. Blood continued to trickle from my wounded vagina. My skin also bore the marks of his merciless handling with angry bruises that mirrored the violence inflicted upon me. My legs quivered beneath the weight of my trembling spirit.

As I stumbled towards the exit, eager to escape the suffocating confines of his wretched chamber, his voice sliced through the air again, halting me in my tracks. The name *"Jade"* fell from his lips like an omen, a chilling proof of the power he held over me. His words slithered with venom, punctuating the command that followed.

The threat hung in the air coiling around my vulnerable heart. *"Do not tell anyone because no one will believe you. If you tell anyone, you will regret it,"* he hissed, planting seeds of doubt in my already tormented mind. His voice went through the room with a promise of unspeakable consequences should I dare to expose the depravity that lurked within these walls.

The truth clawed at the confines of my silenced voice, begging for liberation, but the weight of his threats, the suffocating grip of fear, threatened to crush the seeds of my resilience before they had a chance to bloom. The battle between my desire for justice and the paralyzing grip of his power waged within me.

I finally tore myself away from his room, carrying the heavy burden of silence upon my trembling shoulders. With each step that I took forward, I was consumed with the fear that what had happened would be condemned to the end of time.

CHAPTER SIX

SECRETS AND SILENCE

It seemed as though the threads of my destiny were woven by someone else's hand. I existed as a mere spectator, powerless to shape the path I walked upon. The depressing and recurring events that unfolded left me yearning for a semblance of control, but it remained forever out of reach. Silence became my refuge, a shield against all that threatened to consume me.

The weight of my grandfather's wickedness pressed upon my spirit, leaving me a prisoner in my own thoughts. Perhaps it was fear that paralyzed my tongue, or the haunting sense of violation that whispered incessantly in my ears. I found solace in the quietude of my sorrow, burying my true self beneath a facade of forced happiness.

How could I be a guiding light for my brother Julian? He was trapped in the destructive spiral of our circumstances? John's once- bright future had become marred by the wounds of our shared

experiences. As much as I longed to help him, I was also a slave to my own torment. My inner demons devoured my strength, leaving me powerless to offer more than a fleeting smile.

Behind closed doors, I battled the ghosts that haunted my existence. I grappled with the demons that tore at my spirit, leaving scars that went beyond the surface. The depths of my agony were a secret I dared not speak aloud, for to give voice to my suffering meant exposing the shattered fragments of my soul. I feared judgment, rejection, and the chilling consequences that my grandfather had vowed to inflict upon me if I dared to defy his dominance.

I remained trapped within the confines of my own silent despair, my heart bleeding in silence, and my spirit yearning for liberation. Each day, I wore a mask of feigned happiness, concealing the truth that lay within. Behind the facade, my true self withered, a dying ember struggling to ignite a flame of defiance.

My grandfather did not stop with the first rape. The initial violation I endured was merely the beginning, a prelude to a twisted

symphony of torment that played out day after day. Every day, my innocence was further shattered, replaced by a harrowing existence as his personal object of gratification.

I became a pawn in his sick game, a plaything to satisfy his insatiable lust. The weight of his dominance pressed upon me, suffocating my spirit and leaving me fragmented and lost. I was trapped in a nightmare of my own making, a nightmare that no child should ever endure.

The relentless attacks of his abuse wore away at the fragile remnants of my sanity. There was no escape, no refuge from the attacks of his perverse desires. I was a vessel for his darkest cravings, a receptacle for his lust. It was a cycle of violence and degradation that repeated itself with terrifying regularity.

The boundaries of time held no meaning for him, as he would summon for me with a cruel command. He reveled in the power he held over me, delighting in the fear that coursed through my veins.

He would force himself upon me and in those moments, I was reduced to a mere object, a vessel to satiate his depravity.

His methods of control grew increasingly brutal. His fists would rain down upon my fragile form until I surrendered to his dominance, until my will to resist was crushed beneath the weight of his blows. Along with each strike, the pain reverberated through my body.

I was broken, both physically and emotionally. This was a man more than twice my father's age. The magnitude of his abuse left me trembling, my spirit battered and bruised. The darkness seemed impenetrable, and I felt utterly alone. The cries for help in the confines of my mind went unanswered, drowned out by the silence imposed upon me by his threats and manipulation.

Every night, my pleas for mercy fell upon deaf ears, met with only his twisted satisfaction. The violation I endured became a never- ending nightmare, a relentless assault on my body, my spirit, and my very sense of self.

Even as I reminiscence on those days, I cannot keep the tears back. Rape is never an easy thing to deal with, it is like being robed on an invaluable possession that we cannot get back. I sadly carry these memories all my life and it shaped me into a perpetually defeated person. I lost all sense of worth and self esteem.

Even now, after so many years of being raped, I remind myself that it all happened in the past, but the pain, the hurt, and the regrets, don't just go away. It remained with me, traumatizing me at every turn, ever compelling me to the depressing place of anxiety and suspicion.

Each day, I carried its weight, an indelible mark upon my soul. Occasionally, the weight of the past threatens to consume me entirely, a formidable burden to bear, capable of extinguishing my spirit.

Almost every night, my grandfather would creep into my room like a predator stalking its prey. A small torch illuminated his sinister

intentions, casting shadows on the walls as he approached. My grandfather's motions were swift and decisive. His strong hands would cover my mouth to silence any protests that might escape my lips.

His touch was suffocating, his grip unyielding, as he forcibly beckoned me from the safety of my bed. In my groggy and disoriented state, I would follow him, the weight of his dominance bearing down upon me with each step.

He led me to his room, the chamber of past violations, where he would unleash his monstrous desires upon my defenseless body. He would rape me until he was satisfied. I could do nothing but endure the excruciating torment he inflicted upon me night after night.

However, every morning, as the world stirred awake, my grandfather would roam the house with an air of nonchalance. He was oblivious to the devastation he left in his wake. I would gaze at him with fear and disbelief.

I was astonished by his ability to feign normalcy, to pretend that the horrors he subjected me to were nothing more than figments of my imagination. It was as if he were blind to the destruction he wrought upon my very being, his conscience shielded from the reality of the monster he had become.

One particular Thursday stands out in my memory, for it was a day when my grandmother was absent from our home. She had embarked on spending time away in the city, obliged to attend the annual conference of her women's group from our local church. Her absence created a void, a void that my grandfather exploited with grave precision.

Those three days without my grandmother's cautioning presence became a relentless aggression of sexual violation. My grandfather sent my brother Julian away, deliberately creating a space where he could unleash his darkest desires upon me without interruption. He abused me physically in those three days more

His words sliced through the air, a cruel mockery of my pain and suffering. In his distorted reality, my torment was nothing more than a source of amusement, a sick game in which he reveled.

"No, Papa, I'm not enjoying this!" I would plead. I hoped helplessly that somehow, my defiance would shatter the illusion he had constructed, that he would see the truth of my anguish. His twisted perception remained unwavering, his arrogance unyielding.

"You're lying! You love it, you filthy little slut!" he would sneer, his voice dripping with perverse satisfaction. The accusation cut deep, ripping through the tattered shreds of my self-worth. How could he believe I was enjoying the way he kept violating me? How could he turn my pain into a sick fantasy?

At a point, I stopped resisting. My body began to grow numb beneath his weight. I surrendered to the horrors that unfolded night after night. What purpose did struggle serve when his dominance remained, when my protests were met with nothing but greater devastation? The realization settled upon me like a suffocating

shroud—I was trapped, a prisoner at the mercy of his lustful desires.

He defiled me, my body a vessel for his twisted pleasure. The sanctity of my being was desecrated with every touch, every invasive act. The pain of the violation mingled with the shame that enveloped me, forming a toxic concoction that poisoned my very existence.

Sonya comes by the house quite often, she was the only friend I had in the neighborhood. She was a sweet girl, and the bond we shared was truly simple and innocent. When she came around, she assisted with any chores in the house, accompanied me on all my errands. These moments often helped me to forget the demons that were eating me up within. Regardless of how close we were, I didn't have the courage to tell her what was going on with me.

Sonya's life seemed to hold the freedom and liberty I could only dream of. Living with her brother, who was often away working, she had a world of possibilities at her fingertips. While I envied her

seemingly endless leisure time, I found solace in our shared routines, particularly our regular attendance at the local church.

Twice a week, like clockwork, we would make our way to the solitary church building that stood at the outskirts of town. It was a quiet place of peace and tranquility, about a mile and a half from my grandparents' house.

One beautiful Sunday afternoon, as we walked home from church, Sonya's words cut through the gentle breeze like a sharp blade. *"Jade, you're becoming fat!"* she exclaimed, her tone laced with playful mockery. I became furious at her words, instinctively defending myself. *"Fat? No, I don't think so,"* I responded, my voice tinged with defensiveness and doubt.

Sonya, never one to shy away from speaking her mind, continued to share her observations. *"Well, I've noticed changes in you too. You seem lazier these days, and you've grown bigger. It's hard to believe I'm actually a year older than you now. You're like*

an adult!" Her words struck me like a ton of bricks, casting doubt upon the image I held of myself.

Her laughter erupted, a wild and unrestrained sound that mirrored the weight of her words. She was mocking my perceived weight gain. At that moment, her words seeped into my mind. Did others perceive me the same way? Were there changes in my body that I was oblivious to? The innocent comment morphed into a haunting question, taunting me with the possibility of hidden truths.

"Or are you pregnant?" Sonya teased with continuous laughter. It was a rhetorical question, meant to amuse, but within its casual delivery, I felt a pang of anxiety. The possibility of pregnancy, at such a tender age and under such circumstances, sent shivers down my spine.

Her laughter became a dagger twisting in my gut. I forced a smile, hiding my anxieties beneath a veil of false amusement. A storm raged within me, questions and doubts colliding in a chaos. As we

continued our journey home, the weight of Michelle's words clung to me like a heavy cloak.

I longed to dismiss them, to cast them aside as mere jest. But deep down, I couldn't escape the nagging feeling that they held a kernel of truth, that I was trapped within a body that no longer felt like my own.

The haunting question, *"Or are you pregnant?"* echoed through my mind, reverberating with a persistent intensity. It burrowed deep within my thoughts, refusing to be ignored. Though my knowledge of pregnancy was limited at that time, I found myself consumed by thoughts of what if. What if there was a life growing within me, silently taking root?

The evidence seemed to mount, impossible to ignore. I noticed the changes in my own body, the way my figure seemed to expand, the gentle curvature that formed in my abdomen. It was as if my belly, once flat and unassuming, had taken on a new shape, a cup-like protrusion that whispered of hidden life.

Anxiety gripped me, twisting my insides with each passing moment. I longed for answers, for someone to shed light on the truth that eluded me. That night when my grandfather came to my room, I was determined to ask him. Maybe he held the key to unraveling the mystery that plagued me.

Without hesitation or resistance, I allowed his grotesque charade to play out. It was not just an act of surrender, but a plea for answers disguised as compliance. Deep down, I yearned for him to reveal the secrets hidden within my body, to explain the changes that seemed to consume me.

He feasted upon my body as usual, thrusting and pounding me recklessly. As his savage hunger subsided, the familiar moment of disposal neared. This time, a force surged within me, overpowering my fear and hesitation. Finally, I blurted without a moment's thought, forth, *"I am pregnant!"*

The revelation hung in the air, a confession laced with
uncertainty. It was an admission that laid bare the fears and
doubts that had consumed me, a plea for guidance in a world
that felt overwhelmingly dark. In that vulnerable moment,
I hoped for clarity, for resolution, even if it meant facing the
unimaginable truth that my body carried a life not
of my choosing.

The room fell silent, my words hung in the stillness. His
eyes, clouded with surprise and curiosity, met mine.
I awaited his response, his intentions remained veiled. As
the seconds ticked, an unsettling realization settled upon
me. Perhaps my desperate plea for answers had fallen on
deaf ears, absorbed by a darkness that thrived on the
vulnerability of others.

A flicker of worry passed fleetingly through his eyes,
revealing a glimpse of the man behind the facade. In that
brief moment, I saw the realization that he too was not
invulnerable to the consequences of his depraved actions.

The weight of his own transgressions loomed over him as a specter of fear that threatened to shatter his carefully constructed world. The vulnerability in his gaze was quickly replaced with a mask of indifference, a shield against the truth that lurked within.

He bluffed, attempting to regain control over the situation. His voice was laced with false authority. *"Do you even understand the meaning of what you're saying?"* he questioned with his words dripping with disbelief.

Undeterred, I pressed on, determined to make him see the gravity of the situation. *"Yes, I do. I've noticed the absence of my period for the past two months,"* I responded. My voice trembled with a mix of fear and conviction.

He grappled with my revelation and I could see his mind racing to find a way to dismiss the undeniable evidence. Finally, he mustered a response, his voice encrusted with skepticism. *"Well, I doubt that. Even though it's not a problem. We'll take care of it. Now get out!"*

The brutality of his nonchalant reaction shattered the remnants of my self-worth, leaving me feeling utterly worthless. The dismissive tone, the casual disregard for the gravity of the situation, tore at my already fragile spirit.

As I turned to leave, his whispering voice thundered behind me with a chilling tone dripping with a foreboding warning. *"Hey Jade, you can't tell anyone about this,"* he commanded. Somehow, I understood exactly what he meant. It wasn't a mere suggestion or advice; it was a clear warning with the threat of unspeakable consequences.

That night, I cried my heart out. The anguish within me poured forth in an uncontrollable torrent, and for the first time, Julian stirred from his sleep, awoken by the sobs of my shattered heart. He came into my room through the darkness and sought to comfort me. *"What's wrong, Jade?"* he inquired. I couldn't find the strength to utter the truth that consumed me.

Throughout the night, he remained by my side. His presence offered a sliver of solace. He persistently pressed for answers, desperate to understand the source of my anguish. I sat there, drenched in tears, unable to find the words to ease his growing concern. In that moment, my silence became a barrier, a fortress shielding him from the devastating truth that had shattered my very existence.

I found myself immersed in a dark sea of despair, where thoughts of suicide danced and began to occupy space within my consciousness. Wild, haunting notions taunted me, whispering that death is surely the only escape from the unrelenting torment. The memories of the horrors I had endured surged to the forefront of my mind, inflicting fresh wounds upon my broken spirit. In that moment, I believed that death could offer respite from the agony that plagued me.

Images flashed through my mind like shards of broken glass, each one a twisted embodiment of my pain. I contemplated stepping into

the path of a fast-moving car, the allure of its destruction beckoning me with a seductive promise.

Perhaps, I could just end it all near a body of water and allow the weight of the water to consume what's left of me. I was thinking of ways to erase any traces of my existence. The darkness consumed my thoughts, entangling me in a dance of desperation.

As I wrestled with these morbid fantasies, I laid in bed with a chilling certainty settling within me. The conviction to end my own life took hold, gripping me with determination. *"That's what I will do,"* the words slipped from my lips, heavy with resignation.

CHAPTER SEVEN

UNPREPARED

I awoke to the calmness that blanketed the empty house the following morning. Only the rhythmic tick-tock of the wall clock and the distant melody of birds singing dared to disrupt the silence. For a moment, I allowed myself to be enveloped in tranquility. Yet, as the seconds passed by, so did the relentless worries and anxieties that choked my breath.

The weight of my memories returned like a flood. Each one carried a heavy load of excruciating pain. I was forced to confront the reality that I remained a helpless prey in the clutches of my predatory and sexually abusive grandfather. At the tender age of sixteen,

I had no formal education, opportunities dashed, and dreams obliterated. My heart ached with the unresolved pain of my father's unsolved murder. I had a wound that seemed destined to fester.

My mother's absence hung over me because she left and never came back. Then there was Julian who was abandoned within the cold walls of a psychiatric institution. My entire life was a symbol of shattered family ties and fractured hopes.

Even Jeffrey, once a reserved and promising soul, had morphed into someone almost unrecognizable. He was arrogant and rude and his innocence was replaced by a bitter demeanor that mirrored our broken world.

On that bed, I wrestled with a life that felt void of meaning or purpose. The days stretched ahead and I found myself lost in my own existence. Each thread of my life seemed to unravel, leaving me drifting in a sea of pain and uncertainty.

Why was it quiet everywhere? Perhaps my grandmother had imparted a quiet decree to let me rest, under the assumption that my ailment was merely physical. If only she could peer beyond the surface and perceive the shattered emotional landscape that I navigated.

With a slow, uncertain movement, I rose from the bed and ventured beyond the confines of my room. Yet, the air seemed to thicken with tension as I was met with the presence of my grandfather loitering in the doorway.

"My little angel, you are awake," his words dripped from his lips. It was unsettling how effortlessly he could shift between the roles of a predator in the night and a master of disguise come morning.

"Good morning," I replied with my voice quivering in the grip of both anxiety and trepidation. I braced myself, fearing that the unfolding scene might eclipse even the worst of my expectations.

"You appear tired, my child," his words fell with an air of false concern, an act of kindness masterfully veiled beneath his practiced façade.

"Yeah, I don't feel like myself." His steps carried him closer to me, and a rush of apprehension coursed through my veins.

The proximity to him seemed to intensify the feeling of impending doom, as if the very air was charged with an electric current of fear.

A chilling unease settled upon me as I realized we were alone in the house. Jeffrey must have accompanied grandma on her early morning departure, leaving me isolated and vulnerable in the clutches of my grandfather's presence.

"Why do you look so restless?" he inquired, his voice carrying a note of scrutiny.

"I am not," I quickly answered, though the quivering of my hands betrayed the falsehood. How could it not? Spending mere minutes alone with my grandfather was enough to ignite a storm of vivid apprehensions lurking behind his façade.

"You must understand that I love you deeply, and it pains me to witness you in this state," his words poured forth with a practiced tenderness, concealing the countless offenses that had transpired at

his hands. It was a peculiar gift he possessed. The ability to obliterate past horrors with a mere flicker of affected compassion.

The nights came with brutal onslaughts of blows and merciless beatings along with his perverse advances. It stood in contrast to the mornings, which he adorned with shallow kisses and the deceptive allure of kindness. That was the man he was, crazy and deranged.

"Go bathe and prepare yourself. I've arranged for a checkup with the doctor. You'll be treated and recover swiftly."
A gnawing suspicion plagued me. I knew that I couldn't fully place my trust in him, no matter how convincingly he painted his intentions. However, what recourse did I have? My life has always been at the mercy of others.

When I was done and ready for the day, I noticed his truck outside awaiting my presence. I locked the door to the house and turned to find his gaze already fixed upon me. A contrived smile played on his hypocritical face.

The ride that day was long and quiet, apart from the noise of the rattling engine. It was as if nature itself mourned the impending disaster that loomed on the horizon.

"You understand that I'll always be there for you, don't you?" His words broke the silence a few minutes into the drive. The very kindness he projected now sent shivers down my spine. It felt like a stark contrast to the cruelty I had grown accustomed to. His past actions and this momentary benevolence created a new level of fear within me.

I was well aware of the disdain he harbored for me, viewing me as little more than a pawn for his twisted desires, an object of his pleasure. However, the prospect of inciting his anger that morning, in my fragile state, was an outcome I dreaded beyond words. So, with a heart heavy and conflicted, I nodded in agreement, though every fiber of my being screamed in protest.

"Jade, my dear, you can trust in me. I won't allow anything to happen to you." He held a shallow reassurance, a dangerous lullaby that threatened to mask his sinister intentions.

"Remember, you mustn't utter a word to anyone about our affairs. Your grandmother has been asking so many questions lately, and I'm curious to know if you've said anything to her," he probed with a deliberate caution, doubling back on his own tracks to ensure I was thoroughly ensnared within his web of deceit.

"No, I haven't," I replied with my words, a mere whisper concealing the turmoil that raged within me. In truth, I knew I had to speak up and tell someone about all that was happening to me. The weight of my secret, heavy and suffocating, hung like a noose around my neck. Those thoughts were dangerous. It was a path paved with uncertainty and terror. For now, I held my tongue.

"Good girl," his response was dripping with wicked approval, as if he was grooming me to embrace the monstrous pact that now bound us. *"This is our little secret, you know. You can't imagine the*

extent of what I'm doing for you at this moment, but one day,

when you're all grown, you'll look back and thank me."

The rest of the journey stretched in silence, but within the hushed confines of the truck, a storm of thoughts invaded my attention. I wanted to break free from the snare that bound me, to shatter the shackles that my grandfather had forged.

The question was, where could I turn? Who could I trust? Ever since my mother left, I had been cast into a world of solitude, a world devoid of companionship or refuge.

The truck eventually came to a halt in front of a small, solitary bungalow. Its appearance gave the impression of a hideout rather than a place of healing. Faded paint adorned its weathered exterior, while an unruly lawn hinted at neglect and abandonment. A sense of desolation clung to the surroundings, casting doubt upon the credibility of any services that might be offered within. A worn sign near the entrance declared, "Welcome to Dr. Wick's Clinic,"

an introduction to a place that seemed more like a haunted house than a sanctuary.

The building itself was an evidence to skepticism, a proof to the questionable nature of its offerings. A narrow walkway branched out to a pair of additional rooms or offices, though it was evident that my grandfather knew exactly where to direct his steps. He knocked gently on the door, and a deep, expectant voice beckoned, *"Please, come in."*

Crossing the threshold, my attention was immediately seized by the sight of a man who seemed to defy any conventional standards of appearance. His demeanor seemed that of a man entirely consumed by his appetite with his belly protruding.

As his gaze lifted to meet ours, a broad grin parted his lips, revealing a gap between his teeth.

"Good morning sir!" he greeted my grandfather with a toothy smile, rising from his seat to extend a hand in greeting.

His actions signaled that he held a place of utmost familiarity in my grandfather's inner circle. He seemed reserved for only a select few, a privilege that hinted at their deep bond.

The anticipation in his expression betrayed that he had been awaiting our arrival. *"Good morning, brother. How are you this morning?"* My grandfather reciprocated the pleasantries.

"Oh, I'm as well as ever, how about you?" *"Not too bad either. I might need a few check-ups later, but for now, I'm fine."* Laughter bubbled forth from both of them, a shared camaraderie evident in their easy banter. It was evident that these two men harbored a ton of secrets, their shared laughter resonating with years of unspoken understanding.

Turning his attention to me, he greeted me with the same shallow smile that graced my grandfather's features.

"How are you, my daughter?" he inquired, his tone carrying a hint of the same mischievousness that seemed similar to my grandfather. I extended my hand, mirroring the gesture, and

replied, *"I'm fine, thank you, sir."* His gaze lingered on me as he held my hand, a gaze that spoke volumes despite its superficial nature.

"Is this the girl?" he inquired, his focus now shifting back to my grandfather while his grip on my hand remained steadfast. *"Yes, she is,"* my grandfather affirmed, their exchange a silent confirmation of my presence in the room.

"Please, have a seat," he welcomed us, gesturing toward the chairs positioned before him. Taking our places, a brief moment of quiet lingered, punctuated only by the rustle of paper as he searched his drawer for a pen. He adjusted his glasses, perching them thoughtfully on the bridge of his nose, before finally addressing me with a gentle smile.

"How are you feeling, dear?"

"Not too good, sir."

"Could you describe your discomfort? Is there any particular area of your body experiencing pain?"

"No specific area, sir."

"Do you experience any pain in your breasts?"

"Yes, just a slight ache."

"Have you felt nauseous, as though you might vomit, especially in the mornings?"

"Yes, I've been dealing with that as well."

"Do you find yourself easily fatigued?"

"I can't say for sure, but I have noticed I've been sleeping more than usual."

"At what age did you start your menstrual cycle?"

"I can't recall the exact age."

"And how old are you now?"

"I'm sixteen."

"Have you observed any changes in your menstrual cycle lately?"

"I haven't had my period for about two months now."

He continued with his line of questioning, seemingly well- practiced questions he had likely posed to countless individuals over the years. He handed me a cup and asked me to use it in the bathroom. After I gave it to him, he took it away and returned quickly. *"Alright then."* Shifting his attention to my grandfather, he stated, *"You were right; she is."*

At that moment, the significance of their exchange eluded me, but with the passage of time, the true nature of their conversation

became clearer. Before that appointment, they had obviously discussed the possibility of my pregnancy, and without any consideration for my wishes, they had apparently come to a decision on the course of action.

Once again, my grandfather's desire to exert control over my body manifested, and whatever agreement they had reached was evidently designed to underscore that point.

"Very well, let's not waste any more time. You know the fee," Dr. Wick's words were directed at my grandfather. *"Yes, understood,"* he responded.

"One more thing, I believe we'll be able to discharge her later today. However, a few hours of monitoring might be necessary before she's released."

"Take whatever measures you need to, just ensure the well-being of my little angel," my grandfather replied, his concern masking his true intentions.

Caught in the midst of these two adults, my destiny seemed to hang in the balance, the privilege of choice stolen away from me. *"Jade, come with me,"* he instructed, rising from his seat. It was only then that I realized there was an adjoining room concealed behind his chair.

I followed his lead, my grandfather lingering behind. Inside, he handed me two tablets of medication along with a cup of water. Then, gesturing toward a small bed, he softly spoke, *"Lie down, Jade. There's no need to be afraid. This medical procedure will help alleviate your discomfort. Trust me."*

Reluctantly, I complied. It was not out of trust, but rather due to the stark reality that my ability to resist was practically nonexistent. The uncomfortable episode unfolded. My undergarments had been gently removed with precision by Dr. Wick. As I lay there, vulnerable and exposed, he thrust something into my body, ensuring its deep placement.

He instructed me to remain in that position for approximately three minutes before I could rise. Then he departed from the room, leaving me alone with my thoughts and a whirlwind of emotions.

From my vulnerable position, I overheard their conversation unfold like a chilling symphony. *"It's completed. We'll just wait for an hour or so to ensure she's ready to leave,"* came the voice, unmistakably Dr. Wick's.

"Thank you, Wick. What would I do without you?" my grandfather replied.

"Don't mention it, brother. Do exercise caution in the future. What's with the bruises in her private area? You must be gentler with that girl, you know?" Dr. Wick's tone took on a note of concern.

"You just ensure you take care of her."

"You have my word. You know you can always trust me with that."

"As it will likely be about an hour, I'll return to get her."

"That works, no problem."

"If circumstances prevent me from coming back today, please look after her. I'll inform my wife that she's been admitted to the hospital and will be discharged in the morning."

"That's not an issue, but remember, additional care comes at an extra cost."

Laughter, dark and ominous, reverberated in the room. "Ah, you and your fixation on money. You know that's not my concern," my grandfather chuckled, the sound dripping with an unsettling blend of camaraderie.

The next sound that reached my ears was the swish of the door opening, and then firmly shutting. The room returned to its brooding silence, yet my mind was now a whirlwind of

comprehension. The pieces of the puzzle snapped into place, revealing the twisted purpose behind my grandfather's actions.

The truth seared through me. He had orchestrated this visit to remove my pregnancy. His concern wasn't my well-being after all. It was his ego and reputation that he safeguarded at any cost. The doctor he led me to might be unlicensed or operating with counterfeit credentials. This was ridiculous.

Tears were my constant companion since my father's passing. They blurred my vision once again. His demise marked the conclusion of my true happiness, a memory that now feels like a distant echo. I stayed on the bed, my eyes fixed on nothingness. My mind traveled back to brighter times, days spent in the yard with Julian and Jeffrey.

The memories of harmonious laughter, the radiant presence of my mother that could light up any room, and my father's nurturing warmth that filled our lives with hope and purpose surged forth.

Yet, I was ensnared within these walls, a captive, as my dignity was being cruelly stripped away.

A sudden onset of sharp, piercing pain gripped my abdomen. My insides and the agony was so intense that it tore from my lips a desperate cry for help. Fear clutched at me as my eyes bore witness to a nightmarish sight.

Thick clots of blood flowed from the depths of my being. *"What's happening to me?"* My mind raced with questions, panic dancing at the edges of my thoughts.

Rising to my feet, I checked myself, my heart pounding as the grim cascade continued down my thigh. Soon within moments, the floor I stood upon bore traces of my ordeal. It was a morbid tapestry of blood.

My clothing was soaked, my body was in anguish. The turmoil inside me whispered that maybe, just maybe, my harshest expectations were misguided.

Perhaps my grandfather had at last chosen a path of compassion, a genuine gesture of care. It was a fragile hope, one swiftly shattered. The sheer volume of blood, a sight so foreign and terrifying, confirmed my mistake.

Never before had I witnessed such a gory scene. The anguish left me gasping for air, drained of vitality. As the world began to blur, an overwhelming exhaustion stole over me, and I surrendered to the black abyss of unconsciousness.

The next time I opened my eyes, several hours had passed and it was almost twilight. Slowly, my eyelids lifted, revealing the soft contours of the room. There, by my bedside, a graceful silhouette graced the scene. It was my mother. Radiance illuminated her features, casting a gentle glow upon her countenance.

A smile adorned her lips, one that seemed to hold within it the warmth of the sun. Her hair arranged in a neat cascade, framing her

face in a familiar elegance. She was holding my hand in hers. Her gaze embraced my weary soul.

"My baby, I miss you," her voice resonated like a soothing melody that had long been absent from my life.

"Mom!" I wanted to shout with a surge of excitement that threatened to burst through my chest. In that fleeting moment, I yearned to embrace her tightly, to feel the warmth of her presence wrapping around me like a shield.

It was as if her arrival signaled the end of my troubles, the start of a new chapter where I could confide in someone who would truly understand.

"Baby girl, I know exactly how lost and broken you are. Be strong for me, darling," her words carried a depth of empathy.

"Mom, I want to get out of this place, I am tired, please help me."

"Stay strong my child. Your dad and I love you..."

Then, as abruptly as her voice had graced my senses, I found myself waking up once more. *"It was just a dream,"* I whispered to myself. The reality of the tiny room washed over me, darkness replacing the vivid dreamscape. The evidence of the procedure had been erased, leaving behind only the memory of the dream's embrace.

I refused to let go of the lingering sense of peace and connection that the dream had granted me. It was as if, even in the darkest corners of my existence, a glimmer of hope had emerged.

Then with so much determination burning in my heart. I made a silent vow to myself. Regardless of the threats that my grandfather wielded like weapons, I would muster every ounce of courage to find my mother. I would tell her about the pain and suffering that I have experienced , no matter the cost.

I waited through the long hours of that night, anticipation mingling with unease as my grandfather's absence lingered. It was only when

the night was edging towards dawn that the doctor entered, bringing with him a humble meal of bread and cheese.

He gently advised me to rest, explaining that something urgent came up and my grandfather's arrival would not be until the following morning.

Sleep eluded me that night. My thoughts were consumed by a longing for my mother. A desire that seemed to infuse me with hope and a renewed sense of strength. In the midst of the lonely darkness, her image became a guiding light, illuminating the path through the hours of solitude.

As morning broke, I felt much better. The pain that had gripped me seemed to have receded, leaving me feeling surprisingly restored and ready to face whatever lay ahead. My grandfather's early arrival was unexpected, and his demeanor was unusual. It was hurried and distant.

I couldn't help but wonder if my absence had stirred concern in my grandmother, prompting him to hasten my return to the household to maintain the facade of our secret.

Curiously, throughout the journey home, my grandfather remained silent. The car ride was quiet, the tension was thick in the air. During the few moments I dared to steal a glance at him, I noticed a look that wasn't typical. His appearance was unsettling, and a shiver of concern ran down my spine as I pondered what might be happening at home.

As we arrived home, an atmosphere of unusual activity enveloped the house. It was bustling with the presence of my family members from the city. Thisgathering felt both overwhelming and strangely comforting. The sense of familiarity mingled with a layer of strangeness, making it a reunion unlike any other.

My grandmother sat surrounded by a cluster of women from our local church, their hushed conversations and supportive gestures forming a protective circle around her. She cradled a piece of cloth

in her hands, her posture reflecting a profound grief that seemed to transcend words.

As her gaze lifted, I locked eyes with her, and the raw pain written across her features sent a shiver down my spine. Her swollen eyes, reddened from a torrent of tears, scanned the faces of the gathered relatives and friends. A heavy silence seemed to stretch between us, laden with unspoken questions and a sense of something horrific.

Still confused and trying to make sense of the gathering, my grandmother's voice broke through with urgency.
"Come here, Jade."

I moved towards her with my heart racing and a knot of anxiety forming in my stomach. I felt a whirlwind of emotions. Confusion, fear, and a desperate yearning for answers. As she held my hands gently in hers, her voice trembled as she uttered the words that I had feared the most. Words that were a cruel confirmation of my worst nightmares. *"Your mother died yesterday..."*

CHAPTER EIGHT

A NEW LIFE

I met Tyler at my mother's funeral, and within a year, we found ourselves spiraling down the winding paths of my most dreaded emotions. I remember how in the somber proceedings, he'd stood steadfastly behind me, as the world paid its last respects.

Once the mourners dispersed, he lingered behind, a quiet presence in the echoes of farewell. I couldn't muster the strength to walk away from that grave, as if the earth's embrace might still yield a revelation that this was all a cruel dream.

The sight of my mother's casket descending into the ground clung to my mind as a haunting image I wished to erase.

When I finally turned to leave, my blurry gaze caught the glimpse of a figure moving among the gravestones. Through tear-soaked eyes, I perceived his striking features. There was something magnetic about him.

He had an attractive energy that piqued my curiosity. Our eyes locked, and I, the girl shattered by loss, and he, an interesting stranger, stood at the intersection of our worlds.

Tyler had such a confident stride. He approached me and wrapped his arms around me in a hug that held both warmth and understanding. In that embrace, a new chapter of my life began.

Tyler became an inescapable refuge, a partner in defiance against life's cruelties. He became my guide to momentarily flee the weight of my troubles. Those initial weeks of our meeting were days of tears, particularly flowing freely whenever Tyler's presence graced

my world. The sensation of losing everything consumed me, erasing all of my hopes and dreams.

More so, I had been reduced to prey. I had been captured in the clutches of my heartless and sex-drunken grandfather, who wielded his sinister desires as if they were his birthright.

His grotesque actions bestowed upon me a twisted, unasked-for legacy of violation. My body and spirit was contorted by the burden of his repulsive transgressions.

Tyler was, however, my lifeline of unexpected comfort. An aura of safety enveloped him. There was an assurance that in his presence, vulnerability was not a weakness but a shared experience. Whenever I was with Tyler my tears transitioned from sadness to tears of freedom. .

Tyler's touch and his words conveyed a different message. It was one of empathy, compassion, and a promise that I was not alone in this darkness. He coaxed my grief to the surface, as if he held the key to the locked chambers of my heart, releasing the pent-up anguish that had kept me in bondage for so long. The times we spent together became an oasis where the horrors of my past temporarily retreated.

He told me it was okay to cry, to let the pain spill forth like an unbroken dam, and he reassured me that my tears weren't marks of weakness, but the trophies of a survivor reclaiming her voice.

In Tyler's presence, the world looked new. He was my safe harbor. I found myself trusting him in ways I had never dared trust another soul before. So with each interaction, Tyler shattered the chains of my silence, and in their place, he sowed the seeds of trust.

One evening, he revealed to me his coping mechanism was a path he navigated through the depths of pain. It was drugs. Patiently, he guided me through the process, teaching me how to measure the balance between relief and danger before indulging.

He shared his knowledge of rolling marijuana, weaving them into sticks of pleasure. His relationship with alcohol was less pronounced, yet he was not averse to it.

His room came alive with hazy swirls of smoke, illuminated by the soft, pulsating glow of a lava lamp in one corner. The air was heavy with the sweet, earthy scent of marijuana, mingling with the tang of the alcohol he'd been drinking.

Tyler and I were comfortably sprawled on the couch, our limbs feeling weightless and our minds adrift in a sea of altered sensations.

Tyler's laughter, which seemed to come from a place far away yet intimately close, resonated with the music playing softly in the background. I watched the clouds of smoke around him as he continued to puff on his joint. .

My very first experience smoking marijuana gave me a feeling of relaxation and undescribable peace.Our surroundings seemed to shift and transform, morphing into a dreamscape where reality and fantasy came together. Colors seemed more vibrant, sounds more vivid, and the passage of time became an abstract concept rather than a concrete reality.

On that fateful day, he chose to share the chapters of his life, and as his narrative unfolded, I found myself ensnared by the threads that connected us. Our shared experiences brought about a feeling of kinship I hadn't anticipated.

His life started with a missing piece. His father was a void that marked the inception of his story. The man who should have stood by his side vanished, evading every ounce of responsibility as his mother carried Tyler in her womb. His mother, a woman burdened by her own struggles, brought two more souls into the world, each fathered by a different man.

She was relentless, always on the move, chasing dreams that seemed to lead nowhere. Then, the inevitable happened; she fled once again, this time with a man she had just met, leaving her sons to deal with her abandonment.

Adversity forged an unbreakable bond among the brothers, each so close in age. Forced to fend for themselves, they united with other young outcasts on the unforgiving streets, where survival meant breaking the law. They took to the dark side. An existence of

defiance became their reality, their loyalty to one another stronger than any other force.

In the shadows of these desperate acts, tragedy struck. One of the brothers was killed. Another was arrested and found himself confined within the cold, cruel walls of the prison. Tyler, seeking refuge from the tides of justice, fled from the pursuing law enforcement to lay low at the countryside where we met.

It was during these stark circumstances that our paths crossed. Tyler revealed to me that our connection breathed new life into him, infusing his weary spirit with the strength to change, to evolve beyond the confines of his past. His words resonated deep within me, kindling a belief that perhaps we were each other's catalysts for redemption, but I was wrong.

At first, drugs were an escape, a way to numb the pain that had taken root in the depths of my soul. The first time Tyler introduced me to that world of altered states, I was hesitant, unsure of what to expect.

However, as the smoke curled around us and the effects started to wash over me, I felt relieved. It was as if the weight of my sorrow had been lifted, even if just for a little while.

One evening, the world outside faded away, and the storm within me quieted down. The pain of my past, the haunting memories, the suffocating grip of fear, all of it seemed to lose its potency under the influence of the substances. I found solace in the haze. It was a temporary relief from the relentless ache that had become my constant companion.

Strangely, Tyler's normalcy masked his addictions to substances. He wielded them with an air of refinement in public, creating an illusion that everything was under control. I accepted his assurances that this was the answer to my pain, that it could silence the torment within me.

The afternoons offered brief relief. I sought solace in Tyler's company. Together, we inhaled thick tendrils of smoke, drifting into a realm where pain dulled, if only for a while.

Soon with Tyler, the pendulum swung to its extreme. The sheer magnitude of my sorrow demanded more. I developed an insatiable hunger for the numbing comfort his drugs offered. I became so addicted to his generous supply, the substances offered me a lifeline to a distorted reality.

In the swirl of emotions, our connection went even deeper. He became my sexual partner but the pleasure was shallow at best. It was a mirage, a masquerade that momentarily dimmed the pain without truly healing it. Our entanglement seemed to forge a bond and an understanding that we could conquer the world.

In those fragile times, it felt as though the world held its breath, waiting for us to emerge from the fog of our own making. The drugs became our secret companions, amplifying the intensity of our connection while blurring the edges of reality. We walked on the edge, held captive by our respective demons, yearning for healing that always seemed to evade our grasp.

After some months, the allure of that escape grew stronger. The more I succumbed to the drugs, the more they became my crutch, my refuge from the storms that raged within and around me.

The initial hesitations gave way to a desperate need. The sensations of euphoria, the detachment from reality, and the sense of being free from my pain became addictive in themselves.

I started to become more dependent on the drugs to face the world, to confront the memories that tormented me. They became the only way I knew how to cope, to survive.

The grip of addiction tightened its hold on me with every passing day. The more I used it, the harder it became to face life without them.

There were moments when I knew deep down that I was spiraling out of control, that I was trading one form of suffering for another. The fear of facing my reality without the crutch of drugs was paralyzing. They had become my armor, my shield against the harshness of the world and the haunting ghosts of my past.

No matter how destructive it was, the promise of that temporary escape was too strong to resist. They provided a semblance of control over my emotions and an illusion of power over my pain. I became confined in their grip, unable to break free, or to imagine a life without their false comfort.

Nevertheless, Tyler's influence had instilled in me a newfound sense of boldness and audacity. Despite the ongoing sexual abuses from my grandfather, a night came when the usual intrusion took a different turn. The air was heavy with the lingering scent of drugs, a temporary escape I sought in altered states.

That night, as his footsteps approached my room in their habitual unwelcome rhythm, I was fully alert. The drugs had sharpened my senses, and the ember of a marijuana joint glowed softly between

my fingers. My disheveled hair framed a face wrinkled with both weariness and defiance.

As he entered, I met him with eyes aflame, their red intensity mirroring the anger that had simmered within me for far too long. In a voice that trembled with anger and confidence, I commanded him to leave.

The shock that registered on his face was obvious. It was a cocktail of surprise and disbelief. It wasn't just the fact that he had likely never fathomed my descent into drugs, but the audacity of my demand that seemed to rattle him to the core.

His uncertain steps brought him closer, and in that moment, a veil seemed to lift from my eyes. The facade of the once formidable and reckless man dissolved, revealing a figure of vulnerability and age.

As he neared, a surge of courage pulsed through me, emboldening me to confront the specter of my torment head-on.

Drawing myself up to my full height, I stood eye-to-eye with him, a storm of rage swirling within me. *"I've been waiting for you,"* I declared, my voice dripping with a potent blend of anger and determination. The room seemed to shrink around us as I refused to cower any longer.

A stern warning dripped from my lips like acid. *"If you come any closer to me, be very clear that this time, I won't hesitate to expose you. Your pitiful existence doesn't scare me anymore."* The words flowed from me like a flood of pinned up resentment finally finding an outlet.

As he attempted to interject, I silenced him with a commanding gesture. *"Keep your mouth shut. Do you truly believe you can

continue to hurt me? Get out you damn devil, get out now!"
My voice resonated with an unshakable resolve, every
syllable screamed of my transformation from being a victim
to a victor.

The room practically reverberated with the intensity of our
confrontation. The look in my eyes must have betrayed the
fire that burned within him. Now having a final gesture of
defeat, he slipped away by the weight of his shame.

However, my life with Tyler reached an unexpected and
tragic end when I received the gut-wrenching news of his
self-inflicted demise by drowning in the river. Tyler killed
himself. While I was aware of the shadows of depression that
clouded his spirit, I had held onto the belief that the drugs
and alcohol were providing the freedom and healing he
desperately needed. Little did I know that beneath his
exterior of courage, a battle was raging that even my
presence couldn't help.

At that juncture, my own life had become entangled with his
in a web spun from addiction and dependency.
The substances he introduced me to had woven their
threads deep within me, making them as much a part of my
existence as the air I breathed.

Tyler was my anchor, my means of escape from the pains
that had relentlessly pursued me. His sudden departure
shattered that fragile equilibrium, leaving me stranded and
overwhelmed with devastation.

The floodgates that I had kept sealed, harboring my emotion
and trauma, were suddenly forced open. Grief, loss, and a
variety of feelings I had numbed with chemicals came forth.
The walls I had built to protect myself from my own reality
crumbled, exposing me to the raw intensity of the pain I had
been running from.

Tyler's absence left a void that no drugs in the world could fill. I was faced with the harsh truth that I had been using him and the substances as a crutch, a way to avoid confronting the demons that haunted me.

CHAPTER NINE

FINALLY FREE

Tyler's death coincided with another dreaded event in my life. My grandmother discovered through a neighbor that my grandfather had been raping her and that she was now pregnant. On that particular evening, my grandmother called me to her room.

As I made my way towards her door, a tide of apprehension swept over me, mingling with a curiosity that tugged at my heart. The weight of the unknown hung in the air.

I walked slowly and the floorboards creaked softly beneath my footsteps as if echoing the rhythm of my racing thoughts. Perhaps my grandmother had glimpsed a sliver of my hidden life that I waged behind closed doors.

As I stood in her room, a flood of emotions hit me. Uncertainty, vulnerability, and a fleeting hope that her call held the promise of understanding and support.

"*Jade,*" her voice spoke softly as our gazes met. As she began to speak, her words seemed to carry the weight of years, laden with a sense of deep concern and compassion.

"*My dear child,*" she started. "*I need you to be honest with me. I think I now know, but had no idea you were bearing such burdens. I can't help but feel like I've fallen short in protecting you.*" Her voice quivered, revealing the depth of her empathy and the weight of her realization.

Caught between a desire to reassure and a flood of emotions, I interrupted. "*Why would you say that? What's going on?*" The question hung in the air as a lifeline tossed between us, a bridge to

span the gap between the unspoken and the revelations that were about to come.

Her response cut through the tension, like a knife through a tightly drawn curtain, revealing the painful truth that lay hidden. *"It's your grandfather, isn't it? He's been assaulting you all this time?"* The words landed like a heavy blow, shattering the fragile cocoon of denial that was deep within me. .

Stunned with her revelation, with a nod, I affirmed the unthinkable truth, forging a connection that transcended words. It was as though her understanding reached across the expanse of my pain, wrapping around me with a comforting embrace.

Her other words hit me like a crashing wave, leaving me unable to find my voice. *"My husband has been molesting you, hasn't he?"*

As the fog of disbelief began to lift, I found myself returning to the present moment, my awareness settling back into reality.

I had a feeling of vulnerability and quiet strength, then managed to nod again. In the wake of my grandmother's revelation about my grandfather's heinous actions, a renewed sense of hope seemed to emerge.

It was as if the truth, painful as it was, had finally shattered the chains that bound me to my past. The weight of secrecy had lifted, replaced by a growing determination to overcome the horrors that had haunted me.

That evening, after that tearful conversation and moments of shared vulnerability, my grandmother gently touched my hand with her eyes filled with sorrow and resolve. *"Jade,"* she began, her voice carrying a gentleness that soothed my wounded soul, *"I want to*

help you find your way out of this darkness. You deserve a chance to heal and rebuild your life."

Her words held a promise to pull me from the depths of despair. She explained that she had reached out to a woman in our local church, someone known for her compassion and dedication to helping those in need.

This woman, Mrs. Thompson, had experienced her own journey of recovery and renewal, and my grandmother believed she could offer guidance on the path to healing.

A few days later, my grandmother accompanied me to the church, where I met Mrs. Thompson for the first time. Her warm smile and understanding gaze put me at ease, and as we talked, I felt an unexpected connection. She shared stories of her own struggles and

triumphs, emphasizing the power of faith and community in the healing process.

Through Mrs. Thompson's support, I gradually began attending church events and gatherings more diligently. My best friend would also go with me and help me get through so much. She was easy to talk to, and always had been.

Now that I no longer had to hide, I was able to be more open. Over time, my grandmother, Mrs. Thompson, and my friend became my pillars of strength.

I now had guidance and unwavering faith. They helped me envision a new life beyond the pain and darkness that had consumed me for far too long. They provided resources for counseling, legal assistance, and education, offering me the tools to rebuild my shattered world.

One quiet evening, as I sat alone in my room, reflecting on my life, the scars of my past still lingered. A glimmer of hope had grown steadily within me, fueled by the support that I now had. My grandfather stayed far away from me as if I had a plague and I was thankful for it.

As I sat there, I found myself drawn to the Bible that Mrs. Thompson had given me. Its pages held stories of redemption and love, and in that moment, I felt a yearning to connect with God. With trembling hands, I opened its pages and began to read, my heart searching for comfort and understanding.

Through the verses and words that spoke to me, I found a renewed sense of purpose. It was as if the weight of my past sins and suffering was lifted, replaced by a sense of forgiveness and grace

that I had never experienced before. The presence of Jesus became real to me, a beacon of light guiding me out of the darkness.

Tears streaming down my face, I knelt by my bedside and prayed a heartfelt prayer, surrendering my brokenness and pain to the one who could truly heal and restore. In that moment, I gave my life to Jesus, entrusting Him with my past, present, and future. It felt like a rebirth, a chance to start anew with a newfound faith and hope.

From that point on, my journey took on a different turn. A new strength that came from my newfound faith, I got completely clean, never depending on drugs or alcohol again, and I pursued my education with a determination I had never known before. Mrs. Thompson's unwavering belief in me inspired me to pursue my GED, and with her guidance and support, I was able to achieve that milestone.

Empowered by my education, fueled by my passion to make a difference, I set my sights on becoming a nurse, just like my mother had been. It was a path that felt like a way to channel my pain into something meaningful and impactful. ,I enrolled in nursing school, determined to turn my aspirations into reality.

The journey was not without its challenges, but with God's grace and the support of my friends and family, I persevered. Then, one evening as I was studying in the kitchen, a knock came on the door.

My grandmother was cooking so my grandfather answered. Immediately upon opening the door, several gunshots were fired and my grandfather dropped to the floor.

My grandmother ran to the door but I sat paralyzed in my seat. *"I won't let you hurt another human being ever again!"* Our neighbor screamed.

It was over. It was truly over. I hate to admit this, but although I had moved on, I felt a sense of relief that I had never felt before. Then I heard my grandmother's voice, *"My God, my God. It is well, it is well with my soul."* I guess we all felt free.

The years of hard work and dedication paid off as I graduated from nursing school, a testimony to the resilience that had been forged within me through the trials of my past.

As I stepped into the role of a nurse, I found purpose in caring for others, a healing process that extended beyond my own wounds. Each life I touched became a reminder of the redemptive power of faith and love, attesting to the transformation that had taken place in my own heart.

Looking back on my journey, I am humbled by the ways in which God's love and grace have shaped my life. From a place of gross darkness and pain, I emerged as a survivor, a vessel of hope for others who have walked similar paths.

Through my faith, education, and the love of those who believed in me, I found a new chapter of life. It was now one filled with purpose, meaning, and the joy of knowing that I can do all things through Christ that strengthens me.

Made in the USA
Columbia, SC
15 September 2023

22934348R00089